UNOFFICIAL *Bridesmaids*

Latasha Henry

www.TrueVinePublishing.org

Unofficial Bridesmaids
Latasha Henry

Published by
True Vine Publishing Co.
810 Dominican Dr. Ste. 103
Nashville, TN 37228
www.TrueVinePublishing.org

ISBN: 978-1-962783-87-3 Paperback
ISBN: 978-1-962783-14-9 eBook

Cover design by F16 Regime
www.f16artsworldwide.com
Projectf16@gmail.com

Printed in the United States of American—First Printing

Dedication

To My Heroes,

My three beautiful and intelligent daughters: You have always been the source of my inspiration in life. Through our experiences I've embarked on a powerful growth journey. Always remember to never let your dreams go dormant and know that "The Sky's The Limit."

Preface:

The room was cold and sterile; dark and lonely. Was this foreshadowing of her life to come? Melissa woke up feeling sick. Her leg was throbbing in pain as was her hangover headache. It was like she was in the middle of a bad dream. The night before had been a big mess, and now she was paying for it. Melissa's heart was heavy with sadness, anger, and regret.

What did I do? she thought, grabbing her throbbing head. The trouble started at her tea party bridal shower, where her friends Mya, Denise, Jahel, and Faith decided to liven up the event with alcohol, turning a happy celebration into a disaster.

Scattered and disjointed memories flooded her foggy mind. Echoes of voices screaming, dishes being flung, and shocked faces.

"I got some choice words for Ms. Cruella!!"

"Fuck you bitch!"

"I'm the woman in his life now. You old decrepit heifer"

Will Jacqueline ever forgive me? she wondered. "She didn't deserve the way I spoke to her." she said to herself trying to recollect what transpired. "Did I kick at her? Oh my God!"

As Melissa lay there in the hospital, she was at rock bottom. Her life had fallen apart. The love she had hoped for was fading away, and the idea of getting married seemed like it might not happen. Had she destroyed her chance at happiness? Would she lose the person she loves and her closest friends?

for was fading away, and the idea of getting married seemed like it might not happen. Had she destroyed her chance at happiness? Would she lose the person she loves and her closest friends?

CHAPTER ONE

Denise

A brief sigh escaped from Denise's lips as she read the last sentence of her case note study. The chair tilted slightly as she leaned back comfortably, running her hands through her hair slowly. It was a relaxing feeling. Her eyes began to close but were quickly interrupted by the feeling of another's hand creeping up her shoulder.

Denise whipped her head to the right, looking up from the corner of her eye to see her co-worker Crystal standing beside her wearing a light blue scrub, with a matching-colored head cover. Her face was ridden with fatigue, the crow's feet below her reddened eyes spoke volumes of the stress and lack of sleep that weakened her.

"I've had a long morning on an empty stomach with no rest for the last couple of hours," Crystal stated, quietly stretching her back to the side. A satisfying crack was heard before she stopped, moaning in satisfaction. "Sounds like you need to eat something soon before you crash and shut down," Denise advised in pity.

"I was just considering going to lunch myself after I finished up my case study, you're welcome to join me if you're still looking for food", Denise added as she rubs her belly in a circular motion, mirroring the look of hunger in Crystal's eyes. "I would love that Denise," she replied. "I'm going to get myself a big bowl of everything and stuff myself till I can't move anymore." Denise laughs at her comment, certain that Crystal would do as she said when it comes to food she has been deprived from.

"By the way, how is that case study coming along?" Crystal added "It's coming", Denise sighs, rolling her eyes to the back of her head. She shakes her head from side to side, trying her best to arrange her thoughts. She was running low on fuel, but she needed to finish up before she could leave.

Crystal noticed the look of exhaustion on Denise's face, it was obvious that her brain would burst out from too much thinking. She decides to redirect the conversation, bringing it back to what was really of importance. "Give me about 15 minutes to get rid of these scrubs and let's meet up in the north hospital lobby, in about umm 20 minutes!" she said while hurriedly walking away, desperate for the comfort the meal would soon provide her.

They exited the hospital lobby using the revolving door and headed up the street one block east from the job to one of their favorite spots they often visited called Bistro's. The food they served there always had a way of making their mouths water every single time. "Would you ladies prefer a table or booth?" the hostess asked as they stepped into the entrance that led to the dining area.

"A booth would be fine" Denise answered as they

made their way towards the tables. After being seated, they were greeted by a waitress who sat two glasses of water on the table with a small white bowl containing lemons and a small pair of silver tongs on top. She proceeded to take their orders and walked away.

Immediately following her absence, they were greeted by a gentleman holding a bottle of wine with one hand, allowing it to rest against a white cloth that laid openly on his arm. "Hello ladies, would you like to sample Bistro's wine of the month?" he asked, his French accent slipping into his words ever so slightly.

They both glanced at each other before responding yes with a smile, knowing that they shouldn't be drinking while on the clock. The man nods in approval and gently pours them each a glass of wine. He bows in greeting and leaves them to their conversation. Crystal picks up her glass and twirls it, loving the smell of fresh wine in her nostrils. She takes a small sip.

"So, are you attending the company's Christmas party this evening?" Crystal asked as Denise grabbed the glass next to her and took a sip of wine. She moaned in satisfaction.

"Yes, I'm going," Denise responded, "I was actually planning on taking an Uber there to stop by before I meet up with some friends a little later in the evening for cocktails, what about you?" Denise asked.

"Yes, of course I'm going," Crystal answers. "Sounds like you got a night filled with much fun," she added.

"Hey, I wouldn't have it any other way" Denise exclaimed with a smile. They both laugh as they raised their glasses to alert the waiter they were ready for a refill.

***

The loud beeping sound of a car alarm cried loudly as Denise grabbed one of her pillows on the bed and placed it on top of her head, hoping to silence the sounds coming from outside. When she realized that there was no hope for her ears or her sanity to tune out the car alarm, she rolled across the bed and stood in a sluggish manner. She made her way towards the bathroom, dragging her legs forward like two logs of freshly cut wood. Her eyes squinted as she pressed the switch on the bathroom wall to turn on the lights, looking in the mirror only to reveal the evidence of her long evening of partying and drinking the night before.

Her eyes were puffy with traces of eyeliner and mascara melting down her face. She reached into the cabinet to grab the make-up remover and began rubbing it on her face in a circular motion, closing her eyes to add some cream to that area. While her eyes were closed, Denise replayed flashbacks of the countless number of drinks she consumed the night before.

Once the rubbing stopped, she twisted the handle on the sink to turn on the hot water. She filled her cupped hands with water and began splashing it upward to rinse the make-up cream from her face. After dabbing her face clean of any residue with her towel, she sighed in appreciation. The feeling of fresh air kissed her face tenderly. The honking had long stopped. She thanked God, knowing full well that the sleep she had wasn't enough. She fell to her bed with the last strength in her body, sleep immediately hugging her like a long-lost friend, gradually taking the fatigue away from her weakened flesh.

CHAPTER TWO

Jahel

Jahel rose from the sink and splashed water on her face several times before grabbing the white towel beside her and submerging it in running hot water. She placed it on her face for a few seconds allowing the steam to soothe and rejuvenate her beautiful brown skin.

After removing the towel from her face, she grabbed her toothbrush and paste from the holder at the end of the bathroom counter. She topped her brush with the paste and stared at herself in the mirror as she brushed her teeth.

Jahel must have slipped into a blank stare for a moment because when her eyes refocused, her husband's face and body appeared in the mirror standing slightly to the right with a big smile spreading from cheek to cheek. He bent his head down and placed a soft and gentle kiss on her shoulder bone.

"Good morning my love," Tyler said as he breathed her into himself.

Jahel paused, bending down at the sink to do a thorough rinse. She used a towel to wipe the excess water and placed a fresh juicy kiss on her husband's lips, smiling right back at him.

"Good morning my love."

"How did you sleep last night?" Tyler asked as he

placed his hands on her waist, turning her around slowly with her back pressed against his chest. They both stared at their reflection in the mirror, loving how they both stared at each other rather than themselves.

He gently placed his chin on her shoulder, rubbing the satin material of her nightgown, and making his way up to her belly as he caressed it with both hands, his gaze zeroed in on her.

"Are you ready for today?" Tyler asked, staring straight at her. Jahel let out a big sigh, not knowing what to say. They both knew that there was much to be said.

"Just relax, everything is going to be okay!" He placed the grip around her waist a little tighter, whispering in her ear "I got just the right medicine to get you real good and relaxed."

"Oh really?" Jahel exclaimed.

"I would love to taste that medicine, honestly." She said while kissing her husband tenderly.

"But you do know we have to be at the clinic by 9 a.m. baby, we don't have time to fool around right now."

Tyler glanced at her with a mischievous smile on his face. "How much time is not enough time?" he asked suggestively.

Being unable to resist the temptation, Jahel grabbed her husband's hand and led it down the center of her nightgown, making him feel the wetness she had for him.

"Well, I guess we'll just have to see," Jahel added seductively, making sure she rubbed herself on his palm, making him moan in appreciation.

Tyler could feel through the gown that his wife was not wearing anything beneath her dress as he'd suspected. He turned her around, making sure that she faced his chest. He cupped the cheeks of her butt with his hands and picked her up, placing her body in a sitting position at the edge of the sink's countertop.

He kissed her on her neck making his way down to her shoulder. The strap of her red night gown fell to the side exposing her right breast to his needy mouth. He placed the next kiss on her exposed breast then glided tip of his tongue across her nipple, enticing a low and satisfied moan. Jahel caressed his head with both hands, pressing her nipple closer to Tyler's face. She released her grip from his head and snaked her way down his pajama pants, tugging at the elastic band around the waist with eagerness. She reached in grabbing his manhood and stroking it. His low moans made her arousal twitch, she needed him.

"Should I put it in?" Tyler begged, breathing harshly in her ear. She nodded frantically, bringing his face in for a kiss. He entered her and a low feral moan escaped her lips in a hiss. They caressed each other passionately, on a mission to reach their climax at the same time, something they both enjoyed doing. Once their peak had arrived, the sensual moans and exhilarating sounds that had filled the bathroom were replaced with deep heavy breathing and the sounds of their hearts beating from their chests with each thrust and each moan that came from being molded together in pleasure. They had both reached their climax, satisfaction clouded their faces.

"I love you," Jahel whispered lovingly with the last strength she had. Her husband pecked her cheek. "I love you too." Before they could share a sealing kiss, the sound of a phone ringing stopped them in their tracks.

CHAPTER THREE

Mya

Mya looked at her phone in disbelief when it began to ring right in the middle of her presentation. She reached for it quickly with a slight apologetic smile. "Please excuse my manners" she begged as she glanced at the screen and silenced the ringing for her own sanity. Mya returned to her presentation pressing the small black button on the device in her hand to change the slide on the projector screen.

"So, as I was saying," she continued speaking, hoping that she had not lost the attention of her audience. After she finished up her last few slides, she concluded the presentation as usual by leaving her group with some "Food for Thought" before exiting the conference room with her phone in one hand and her black leather business binder in the other.

Mya made her way down the hall to her office. She entered the room and sat the items in her hand on top of her desk. Her phone flashed silently while vibrating violently on the table to alert her that there was yet another call coming through that needed her attention.

She flopped down on her plush white leather desk chair before grabbing the phone, and answering it in a concerned voice. "Hey Aunt Erma! What's going on, is everything okay?"

"Chile, I was just about to ask you the same thing!" responded Aunt Erma. "I've reached out to you several times in the last two weeks, trying to ensure that you were safe and okay, but you never answered or returned my calls."

"My apologies Auntie, I've just been busy with work. I have a lot of projects that I have to manage right now, and it's been consuming a lot of my time over the past month."

"Chile I was one step away from booking a flight to New York even though I'm terrified of planes, but that was a chance I was willing to take to ensure my Niecy Pooh was okay."

"I'm good, Auntie. You don't have to worry." Mya could tell by the sound in Aunt Erma's voice that her concern was deeper than what she led her to believe, and it was confirmed when she asked. "So how have you been doing since the breakup with your old man?"

Mya's eyes began to tear up instantly. She took a deep breath before responding softly. "Everything is good. I've just been keeping busy. No worries!"

"Okay Hun, I just wanted to make sure you were okay. I know you had a hard time dealing with the aftermath of the situation. You're all alone out there in New York. You should consider coming back home to visit soon. I think it would be good for the soul and just to take some time out for yourself. You can't stay busy forever!" Aunt Erma said.

"I would consider it Auntie, but I have to go now. I'm getting ready to go into another meeting," Mya responded.

"Okay, Niecy Pooh. Just remember what I said. You can't stay busy forever! I love you, and I'll talk to you soon,"

"Okay, I love you too."

Exhausted, Mya leaned back in the chair, relieving the aching pressure from the constant standing and walking around. Her alarm rang signifying another meeting was ready. She stood to leave the office with her things bundled up in the comfort of her arms when her phone began to buzz.

CHAPTER FOUR

Faith

The phone rang for the third time before Faith answered.

"Hello!"

On the other end of the line was a deep and masculine tone of a man's voice. "How's my beautiful lady today?" A smile spread across Faith's face as she answered.

"Wonderful, and how has your day been Mr. Handsome?"

After quickly briefing her on his long and busy day, he concluded the conversation with a question. "Are you available for dinner tonight around 8:30 p.m.?" He asked in anticipation. Faith paused for a second as she racked her brain to check her schedule.

"I think that will work for me. I should be finishing up with my last client's hair around 7:00 p.m., which should give me enough time to shower and get dressed." She responded. "What restaurant are we meeting at?" she asked.

"The Premiere on Fifth Ave," he responded.

"Oh, and it would be great if you could take an Uber there because I wanted to check out a nice spot I heard about from one of my business associates today. He said it's a great place to get good drinks, dance, and the crowd is a vibe. We can just ride there together in my vehicle after we leave the restaurant."

She responded with excitement "Ok, that sounds good, I'll see you in the next few hours."

"For sure," he responded.

Time had passed by so fast, Faith looked at her watch, making sure she greeted everyone "Good night" before she closed up for the evening, locking the door behind her last client. It was 7:23 p.m. She shut off the lights to the salon, rushed up the stairs quickly to her conjoined loft-style apartment, and headed straight for the bathroom. She had exactly one hour to shower, get dressed, fix her hair, and put on make-up. She still had to grab an Uber over to the restaurant. Faith giggled to herself as if she already knew that this was an impossible task, but she was definitely up for the challenge.

***

The Uber pulled up to the restaurant at exactly 8:47 p.m., the driver clutched the handle on the back door of the black Sedan and opened it, allowing Faith to step out. Her nude red bottom stiletto heels clicked against the pavement as she exited the vehicle and made her way to the entrance of the restaurant walking in a fast-paced strut.

There was a bright neon sign that displayed the name of the restaurant, *Premiere*. Once she entered the building, she saw Kevin wave to catch her attention. As she walked towards him, he stood up and pulled out the chair sitting across from him for her to be seated.

"I started to think you weren't going to make it or should I say leave me hanging," Kevin said with a smirk on his face. Faith smiled as she sat down.

"I went over my time limit with my last hair client, which left me with very little time to get ready, but I managed and I'm here now," she responded.

"Yes, you are, and you look beautiful," he responded. "I would ask if you've had a busy schedule today, but I already know based on your arrival time."

Faith gave him a bashful smile because she knew he had a pet peeve for tardiness just as well as he knew that her schedule can sometimes be unpredictable, but she ignored his comment, shifting his mind to another conversation.

"So how long will you be in town on your business journey?"

Before he could respond the waiter walked up with a gold bucket filled with ice and a bottle of champagne sitting inside it. "As you requested," stated the waiter looking in the direction of Kevin as he placed the bucket in the center of the table. The waiter sat two flute glasses right next to it. Faith looked at the items with a surprised expression. "What's the special occasion?" she asked.

Kevin leaned forward and extended his arm to remove the bottle of champagne from the bucket. He began removing the foil wrapping from the tip, gently pressed the cap, and popped the bottle. A foggy mist was released as he grabbed each glass one at a time and tilted it to the side, he poured the liquid until both glasses were half full. Kevin handed one glass to Faith and kept the other one for himself. He raised his glass to initiate a toast. "To long days and short nights."

She raised her glass in return with a soft smile, welcoming his little speech.

"Cheers," she said as their glasses clinked together in unison.

CHAPTER FIVE

Melissa

Their glasses touched together creating a clinking sound before making its way to their lips. Melissa glanced around to observe the private dining room area they occupied. It was the exact restaurant that they had dined at for their first anniversary, which was one of their most unplanned celebrations that became a very special and intimate night they'll never forget.

The ambiance was a soothing tone as usual. The room was dimmed with lighting provided by candles. A brick fireplace was center-lined on the back wall colored with a soft gray lacquer paint. The burning fire brought a soothing glow to the room. The table they sat at was covered with a white tablecloth and was topped with deep dark red rose petals scattered across it. It was romantic.

Melissa's observation was suddenly cut off by the sound of Stephen's voice as he began to speak. He was holding a medium-sized box wrapped in elegant sparkling silver paper and tied perfectly with a white satin ribbon on top of it.

Melissa's eyes widened with surprise and panic as her brain scrambled, trying to remember a conversation regarding exchanging gifts during dinner on Christmas Eve. After reassuring herself that was not the previous agreement a twisted smirk appeared on her face as she squinted her eyes at him.

"I wasn't aware that I should have brought my gift for you to dinner tonight," she said as she drew out the pattern of an invisible question mark in the air suggesting a response.

Stephen smiled at her, shaking his head.

"No that was not our agreement, but because you are such an amazing woman, I thought now would be a great time for you to receive at least one of your gifts a little early since you've been a good girl this year!"

"One of my gifts?" Melissa asked with a big smile filled with excitement as she reached for the box, immediately pulling the bow apart and removing the perfectly wrapped paper. Once she was done unwrapping, sitting on the table was a black box, she slowly removed the top lid to find another box smaller than the one she had just opened. When she pulled it out of the box, she noticed it was wrapped the same as the previous box.

Without saying a word Melissa began to open the second box. Once it was uncovered there sat another black box that she slowly removed the top lid to find another box smaller than the one she had just unwrapped. Once the third box was unwrapped, she removed the top, and inside it was a small fluorite crystal rock that reflected the shades of purple, blue, green, and gold.

Underneath the rock was a small white piece of paper folded into a small square shape. She grabbed the paper and held it up, while softly shouting "Really." She looked up at Stephen who watched her with a devilish smile hoping not to disturb any of the other guests dining in the restaurant.

"I can't believe you made me unwrap all these beautiful boxes to get to a rock and one little piece of paper." Stephen sat quietly and admired Melissa as she made a little fuss about how many trees were used to make the paper that she had just ripped to shreds.

"Well at least it can be recycled," he replied teasingly.

Melissa gave him a quick squint with her eyes before she carefully unfolded the piece of paper at least four times before it was completely opened. Her eyes began to scan across the words as she read.

"Since the day our eyes met, there was something special I saw within them, and over the years, you have brought continuous life to that moment. Each of the three boxes that you unwrapped tonight signifies a layer of shield that covered my heart. The first layer uncovered my flaws and insecurities, the second layer contained the support and encouragement provided by you, and the third layer included the love and security you have shown standing by my side. The fluorite crystal rock that was placed on the top of the paper is the color of love you bring to our relationship, and the placement of the two represents how you hold me down no matter what. You are my rock, and I love you, Melissa."

Tears trailed down from Melissa's cheeks as she

lifted her gaze towards Stephen, who was holding a small black box in his left hand. His right hand held the box open, exposing a beautiful princess-cut diamond ring. More tears began to fall from her eyes as she heard the words come out from his lips.

"Will you marry me?" he asked nervously.

Melissa wiped the stray tear from her face, nodding her head with a small smile in approval, too shocked and speechless to speak. Stephen slowly slid the ring onto her finger.

"A perfect fit," she said in a proud and honored tone.

"Yes, a perfect fit just like you are for me." He leaned over the table to welcome his new fiancée with a kiss as cheers and applause generously filled the room. The deal was sealed.

CHAPTER SIX

The Appointment

(JAHEL)

Jahel and Tyler sat in the lobby area filled with a few other couples making small talk as they waited for their name to be called.

Tyler placed his hand on Jahel's thigh to calm down the nervous shake in her leg, "Don't worry everything is going to be okay" he said. Jahel closed her eyes for a brief moment and let out a sigh of temporary relief. The white door next to the receptionist's desk opened and there stood a woman in a rose-pink scrub uniform with a chart in her hand. She glanced down, looked up and called out, "Tyler and Jahel Summers? We are ready for you now."

Tyler took his wife's hand and led her to the door where the woman waited for them. As they approached her she directed them to the left.

"Please follow me this way. The doctor is waiting to see you."

They entered the room and saw Dr. Flemming sitting at his large handcrafted oak desk. This was the same desk his father sat at when Tyler used to come to visit Dr. Flemming Sr., his childhood physician.

Unlike his father, Dr. Flemming specialized in gynecology and andrology, the study of both male and female fertility, reproductive testing, and treatment.

"Please have a seat," Dr. Flemming said as he stood up halfway out of his seat and pointed to the two chairs sitting on the opposite side of his desk. Once they were seated he began to speak. "I submitted samples for you both to be tested a week ago. We received the reports from our lab, so I wanted to bring you both back in as soon as possible to go over the results."

Jahel and Tyler turned and looked at each other, interlocking their hands while sitting quietly as he spoke. He opened the chart in front of him.

"Mr. Summers, I will begin with your results. Based on the test we were unable to find any underlying issues that would prohibit you from being able to reproduce." Doctor Flemming said.

"Thanks doc, that's great to hear." Tyler blurted out eagerly, unable to conceal his happiness. Jahel grasped her husband's hand tighter as Dr. Flemming began to discuss her results.

"Jahel, the report from your test results and hysterosalpingogram x-ray examination indicates that there is a blockage in your fallopian tubes, which is preventing a successful passage for your eggs to connect with the sperm or allow fertilized eggs to reach the uterus."

Jahel's eyes immediately filled with tears as she turned and looked at her husband with sadness in her eyes.

"Before you get discouraged, there are some nonsurgical and fertility options available that you both may want to consider to increase your chances of conceiving a child," said Dr. Flemming.

"What options do we have, doc?" Tyler asked.

"I was just about to go over the details of each option," Dr. Flemming responded. "There are procedures that could be done depending on the location and extent of the blockage in the fallopian tubes. For instance, there's a nonsurgical procedure to clear the blockage called fallopian tube recanalization known as FTR," he stated.

"What will be my chances of getting pregnant after this and what are the effects if any?" asked Jahel as she leaned forward in her seat anticipating his response. Dr. Flemming continued explaining.

"After the procedure is done, your chances of becoming pregnant will depend on a few factors; your age, if there was any damage to your tubes, and the potency of your husband's sperm. There are chances of you getting pregnant, but there's also a high risk in the possibility of it being an ectopic pregnancy which can be very dangerous to you and may cause serious complications."

"The next option available is through in vitro fertilization known as IVF, this treatment consists of collecting eggs from your ovaries and your husband's sperm which will be sent to the laboratory where they will be linked together. This process takes about three to five days for a healthy fertilized egg to be developed, then the embryo will be placed into your womb to grow into a pregnancy."

"Is this painful?" Jahel asked with concern.

"Not too much pain, just some minor cramping afterward, the whole procedure takes less than thirty minutes and is done with a very thin needle used to aspirate the eggs from the ovaries." Dr. Flemming said, hoping to bring comfort regarding her concerns.

"There are a series of hormonal stimulant injections that will need to be administered at home daily for about ten to twelve days to help your body produce more mature eggs to be fertilized. After the embryo has been transferred to your uterus, you will be required to take daily hormone progesterone shots for eight to ten weeks to prepare the lining of the womb so the embryo can attach," he added. "This sounds pretty intense, doc. I'm sure this type of procedure comes with a healthy price tag!" Tyler said, waiting for Dr. Flemming to respond.

"Because IVF requires multiple stages of preparation and after-treatment, the average cost can range between eleven to thirteen thousand dollars. Depending on your medical insurance company they may be able to provide some coverage support for testing and treatments."

The room went silent for a moment, Jahel had a fearful look on her face after taking in all the information that was just provided. Dr. Flemming broke the awkward moment of silence and concluded the visit.

"I know this has been a lot for you both today and I recommend that you take some time out to thoroughly discuss your options before making a decision. When you're ready, just give the scheduling nurse a call to set a follow-up appointment with me."

"Thanks, doc, for all your help," Tyler said, holding his wife's hand as they exited the office.

CHAPTER SEVEN

The Morning After

(Melissa)

Melissa was awakened by a kiss on the lips. Stephen sat on the edge of the bed with his hand placed on her hip. Melissa opened her eyes with a smile as she released a satisfied hum from her mouth. She grabbed the satin sheets on the bed snuggling them closer to her naked body.

"Good morning, I'm surprised to see you up so early before me. That's pretty unusual for you!" she said.

Stephen chuckled. "Well today is not your usual day. We are now engaged so I thought that I would start the day off differently by making my fiancé a nice hearty breakfast in bed."

"Ooh, I'm enjoying the unusual you already!" Stephen smiled in return, reaching over to take the serving tray from the nightstand on the side of the bed and placed it on Melissa's lap.

"Aww! baby this looks amazing, and it smells good too!" she said, her eyes twinkling as she looked at him in admiration of his generosity.

On the tray was a plate filled with scrambled egg whites, topped with sliced tomatoes and avocado. On the other side of the plate was a small white bowl with strawberries, grapes, and blueberries. The breakfast platter was completed with an eight-ounce glass of water and a clear vase with a single red rose. It was beautiful.

As Melissa began to eat her meal she signaled to Stephen. "Hey babes, can you put my phone on the charger? It's dead and I want to call my parents and tell them the great news."

Stephen grabbed the phone off the nightstand, connected it to the charger, then turned around to face Melissa.

"I know that last night was a special moment for the both of us, but can I ask a small favor of you?"

"What is it babes, is everything okay?" she asked.

"What I wanted to ask is that can you keep the engagement between us until I break the news to my mother first?" he begged.

"When she was very sick battling cancer, I always promised her that when the time came for me to propose, I would be sure that she was there to witness the moment."

Melissa's eyes widened in disbelief as the fork she was holding froze in midair. She raised her voice in a high-pitched tone and shouted. "What do you mean? Will you propose again or something?" He kept quiet, confirming her suspicion.

"A small favor? You're kidding me, right?" She scoffed in disbelief. "That doesn't mean my parents can't know about this… Or does it?"

"I'm sorry Melissa. She has to know first."

She could tell by the expression on Stephen's face that this was not a joke. There was complete silence in the room. Melissa removed the tray from her lap and placed it on the nightstand, gathering the covers and wrapping them around her as she rose from the bed and made her way to the bathroom with tear-filled eyes.

Melissa couldn't believe the conversation that had just occurred between her and Stephen as she slammed the door. This made her think back to the first time she had met Stephen's mom, Jacqueline. They had been dating for nearly three months around that time. Stephen invited Melissa out to dinner at one of the five star restaurants owned by his family.

Upon her arrival she witnessed a woman off to the side chastising a man who appeared to a busboy at the restaurant.

"I'm sorry Jacqueline, that won't happen again!" she heard the man say.

"I know it won't happen again, and by the way, that's Miss Jacqueline to you!" She responded in a snooty tone as she cut her eyes to the left, placing them directly on Melissa.

"And how can I help you?" Jacqueline asked coldly, looking as if Melissa had been eavesdropping on her conversation.

Taking a deep breath before responding, Melissa responded, "Hello, I'm Melissa, and you must be Stephen's mom," she said as she extended her hand to greet her. Jacqueline disregarded Melissa's gesture, looking her up and down from head to toe making a full observation.

"Here we go again, Stephen!" Jacqueline mumbled underneath her breath as she led Melissa towards the back of the restaurant prancing in her well-dressed linens as if she was a runway model.

CHAPTER EIGHT
A New Day

(MYA)

Mya woke up this morning a little earlier than normal. The sun rays glared into her room, peeping through her khaki-colored room darkening shades.

She lifted her head and glanced over at the alarm clock that sat on the nightstand next to her bed. The big red block format numbers read 7:24 a.m., which she thought was too early for her to be waking up on a Saturday morning.

Mya lay stretched out on her bed for another twenty-five minutes before she made her way to the kitchen to brew a fresh pot of coffee--her day starter. She grabbed a measuring cup from the cabinet along with the coffee grains, creamer, and sugar as she thought about how she always tended to make more cups of coffee than she needed being that she lived alone.

As the delightful aroma from the coffee pot began to fill the room, Mya made her way toward the balcony window and pulled back the shades.

The sunlight shone in directly through the window causing each of the plants in its view to rise and dance as she watered them. After watering the plants, Mya grabbed her cell phone to check the time, it was 8:15 a.m. She decided that she would give her childhood friend a call to inquire about an open hair appointment for today. The phone rang a few times before she heard the sound of a woman's voice on the other end speaking in a slow and raspy tone.

It was Faith who always seemed to sound so terrible when she was unexpectedly awakened from her sleep.

"I see your morning greeting is still the same impression of old man Nelson." There was a brief moment of silence on the phone before both ladies burst out hysterically in laughter.

A feeling of nostalgia swept their hearts as they remembered the sound of their third-period geometry teacher's voice back in high school as he recited the notes for their weekly tests that no one ever seemed to understand.

After a quick run-down memory lane, Faith informed Mya that she had an open appointment slot for two o'clock if she wanted it.

"Great, that will work for me, and we can finish chit-chatting then," she replied. Mya hung up the phone and took one last sip of her coffee before changing into a pair of pink and black yoga pants with a matching sports bra. She grabbed her sneakers and headed out to the gym.

***

"What a stress reliever," Mya said as she exited the gym.

There's nothing like a good workout to get you all sweaty and energized, she thought, while walking to her car. Going to the gym was not just for exercising and staying in shape for Mya, but it also provided time for her to let all things go while putting power to her grind.

Mya chuckled to herself when she thought about the excruciating look that was on her face as she counted down the last ten seconds of holding her plank. She distracted herself by singing to Rihanna playing in her "Beats" cordless headphones. "Work Work Work Work Work!!!" She sang.

What a sight to forget, she thought, shaking her head as she left the gym, heading to her car. She hit the unlock button on the key fob, jumped in the car, and started the ignition. She reached for the rear-view mirror to take a look at the sweaty hair damage that was caused by her workout. It was 10:52 a.m., and she still had a good two and a half hours left before she had to meet with Faith for her appointment, which she desperately needed. Mya lifted her arm rest and pulled out a fitted baseball cap she usually kept in the car for bad hair days like this and placed it on her head. She adjusted the strap in the back, took one more glance in the mirror and decided to use her spare time shopping at the mall to get some new items for the night.

CHAPTER NINE

All About Me

Mya turned on Catsberry Lane, a long road that led to a brownstone brick driveway. As she pulled into the driveway, her view was directed towards an array of cars lined up alongside the garage which gave her the impression that Faith had added a few new cars to her automobile collection.

This was something she enjoyed doing since she first got her license to drive. Mya found an available spot and parked. She grabbed her bags and exited the vehicle. Once she arrived at the back door that led to the lower level, she rang the doorbell sounding three chimes. When the chiming of the bell stopped, she heard a purring sound coming from the other side of the door. The purring sound stopped when Mya rang the bell for the second time.

As she looked around, she noticed that there was a motion-detecting camera over her head that pointed down focusing on her every movement.

The sound of footsteps drew her attention back towards the door as Faith's face appeared in the square glass window of the back door. The door opened and they both embraced each other in a big hug.

After their greeting, they turned and walked down the stairs that led to the open area where Faith ran her beauty salon. It was visible to see that the space appeared to be the same as it was the last time she came by for an appointment about six months ago. There was one styling chair that sat in front of a large circular mirror trimmed with bright mini-light bulbs. Two overhead dryers sat side by side against the wall at the back of the room, adjacent to them was a matching apple-colored washer and dryer set.

In the corner sat one chair for a waiting client. Faith wasn't too big on having too many people in her salon at once, so she kept the seating very limited. Mya scanned the walls, admiring the creative art canvases that Faith had collected during her travels around the world for platform hair shows.

From the look on Faith's face, Mya could tell that she began to recognize the scent of a familiar smell lingering in the air. Before Faith could say a word Mya reached into her black leather shoulder tote and pulled out a white paper bag.

On the front of the bag was a bright yellow circle and inside of it was an image of two chili peppers, one green one red, and both wearing brown cowboy hats. Faith's eyes widened, screaming out "Taqueria Tacos! I haven't had their food in ages!"

She grabbed the bag frantically from Mya's hand and flopped down into one of the dryer chairs.

Faith was amazed to see that her friend still remembered the exact way she ordered her tacos back in the day. She reminisced on how she would step up to the counter in the same sequence every time and say, "three steak tacos on corn tortilla shells with rice, beans, cheese, cilantro, onions, lettuce, tomatoes and please put limes and peppers on the side."

Faith assured Mya that she would have to eat at least one taco before she could get started on her hair. Mya gave her the okay as they began to talk and catch up on the details of their lives. Faith elaborated on several new adventures she had been exploring, traveling frequently to L.A. and Miami, to network as she expanded herself to new business opportunities. Mya was always excited to hear her adventurous stories filled with lavish experiences that included dining, shopping sprees, parties, and multiple celebrity encounters she had.

Mya began explaining to Faith how she had been so busy, and consumed with work and school. She had just entered into the program to complete her doctorate degree.

"Girl, I seldom have time to go downtown anymore to enjoy myself. I want to make the best of this work-free weekend."

"Today I have three events to attend!" Mya said as she grabbed her shopping bag off the floor, pulled out the clothing items, and flaunted them around awaiting Faith's approval of her pieces.

After two hours of swapping stories, the beauty process was finally completed. Faith spun the chair around, facing the mirror as soft beams from the lights cast down on Mya's hair, revealing a sleek shine with tremendous flow. Faith smiled as Mya nodded in agreement after being asked if she was satisfied with her services.

"Yes, girl! You have given me the best! Can you see those curls?" she asked in disbelief, dragging out her words.

This shoulder length softly curled bob was the perfect style Mya needed to pull off her evening that was filled up with multiple events.

Mya handed Faith her credit card. "Don't forget to give yourself a nice tip," she said. The ladies hugged and said their goodbyes. On the drive home, Mya smiled excitedly thinking about her plans for the night.

CHAPTER TEN

The Weekend

It was Friday, a day that Denise valued the most out of the week because that meant it was officially the weekend.

"I can't believe that today is finally our last day of residency," Denise said with excitement as she raised her hands over her head in the shape of a "V" to represent victory, exhaling a grateful sigh of relief.

"I know, right? I can't believe it's been three years now since we first met. Time is flying!" Crystal replied.

"It seemed like just yesterday when we were standing in this same hallway with several other residents dressed in scrubs, with those stuffy lab coats!" Denise said in irritation.

"Yeah!" Crystal agreed, "I always lost my stethoscope even though I always hung it around my neck!"

"We were so eager to hold those clipboards in our hands, so eager to begin our medical journey of conducting research, attending lectures, and completing medical exams! But now look at us, tired and underfed!" Crystal added dramatically.

"And the list goes on!" Denise interrupted nonchalantly, shaking her head to alert Crystal not to remind her of the overwhelming process it has been these last few years.

"Ok, ok I get it. I'll let you enjoy this moment in peace," Crystal responded with a warm smile as she nudged her shoulder. Denise nudged and smiled back.

"So, what are your plans for celebrating this weekend?" Crystal asked.

"I don't have any pre-planned engagements. I've been so exhausted lately. I was just going to honor my accomplishment by focusing on doing some self-care this weekend and preparing for the board exam scheduled for Monday afternoon. I've already booked a spa day appointment at the Comfort Zone tomorrow to pamper myself with a massage, facial, manicure, and pedicure, then go home to watch Netflix and chill with a bottle of wine after a soothing Epsom salt bubble bath."

"Sounds peaceful and relaxing!" Crystal said in admiration.

"I expected you to be out partying and drinking with your friends to celebrate," she stated.

"Well, in honor of my success, my sisters and I are going to the bar for drinks tomorrow evening after dinner. If you decide to change your mind or if watching Netflix alone gets too boring for you then you're more than welcome to join us," she added.

"Don't threaten me with a good time! I just might consider taking your offer," Denise replied.

They both made their way to the conference room where they joined the other residents, interns, and medical students to celebrate the completion of their residency program with a cake provided by their attending physician. They were so happy and blessed by his presence and the glorious snack.

***

"Which no chip polish would you like for your manicure and pedicure?" asked the nail technician as she handed Denise a color wheel with the various polishes they offered.

"I think I'll try number 514," she responded.

"Oh, the honey beige," the woman said, pointing to the color on the wheel.

"This is one of our new colors, you're going to love it," she said with confidence.

After being reassured by the woman that she had made a good choice in color. Denise sat comfortably in her white robe and matching head towel, items that she was previously given to wear during her massage and facial session. She hit the recline button on the spa chair to get in a relaxed mode as she leaned back to enjoy this experience as well.

Denise closed her eyes as the scent of lavender oils lingered throughout the room and the sounds of stress relief meditation music played on the surround sound system putting her in a restful state.

***

Everything for Netflix and chill was set. Denise had

her popcorn, chips, peanut M&M's, a bottle of Red Romance, and a wine glass spread across the cocktail table in the living room. She plugged down on the couch and grabbed the television remote that was sitting beside her. She clicked the power button and scrolled down the selection of movies twice before she hit the play button choosing one of the movies from the drama category.

Denise was about forty minutes into the movie and halfway through her bottle of wine when her phone began to buzz. She looked at the screen to see a text from Crystal reminding her of the invite for drinks. Denise turned her head back towards the TV ignoring the message and continued watching the movie.

Ten minutes later, the phone began to buzz again. This time she picked up the device and opened the message. It was a picture of Crystal and her two sisters toasting drinks at the bar.

The caption of the photo read "Wish you were here to celebrate with us," followed by a cocktail, confetti, and sad face emoji. Denise couldn't resist noticing the excitement on their faces indicating that they were having a great time.

She threw the phone down on the couch, paused the movie, and headed to her bedroom to get dressed. She realized that she was not going to miss out on a good celebration. It was a Saturday night. She would have time tomorrow to rest and study before the state board exam on Monday.

***

Plink; plink; plink;

The sound of water droplets falling one after another echoed in Denise's ear. Her eyeballs moved underneath her eyelids as she struggled to open them. Her eyes cracked letting in the blurred, painful light of day.

"Ow!" Denise groaned as she tried to rise from her lying position. She felt a sudden pain flow through her body. She sharply rose to a sitting position looking disoriented and confused, wondering where she was. Her foggy vision cleared to reveal a stainless steel toilet with a dripping sink right next to it. When she looked down, she noticed that her excruciating back pain was caused by the cot bed she was sitting on. She was in a jail cell but didn't have a clue why.

"Hey, it's time to go," yelled the officer while banging on the steel bars with his billy club.

"What?" Denise responded.

"Oh, I see you've finally come to your senses. You were all messed up when they brought you in last night!" said the officer.

"What?" She repeated in a confused state. "I don't understand!"

"Time to go," the officer said again. "The judge will explain everything when you appear before him."

Denise was taken to a small courtroom upstairs from the holding cell. When she entered, she was instructed to stand at a wooden podium. "Raise your right hand" the bailiff ordered. "Do you swear to tell the truth, the whole truth, and nothing but the truth?"

Dazed and confused, Denise complied, "I… do."

The judge proceeded to open her file and began reading. "The perpetrator was severely intoxicated and became combative with an Uber driver and two additional passengers. The perpetrator made insulting remarks and threats while using derogatory language. The perpetrator physically attacked the Uber driver and damaged his property, which referenced the Uber driver's vehicle."

Denise's eyes widened in disbelief.

"How do you plead?" the judge asked her.

She hesitated. "Your honor, I am unaware of myself displaying those actions stated by you. Is there any way I can get a lawyer to represent me at my next court appearance?"

The judge turned his head to the prosecuting attorney and asked if they would be in agreement for a continuance on this case.

After the deal was made, the judge labeled the charges as assault and battery and ordered for the bail amount was to be set at ten thousand dollars and stated that ten percent of that would need to be paid before Denise could be released from custody. The officer walked up and signaled for her to follow him back to her cell.

"You get one phone call. Would you like to use it

now or later?" He asked as they proceeded down the hallway.

"I would like to make that call now!"

CHAPTER ELEVEN

The Announcement

❝I just started a fresh pot of coffee to jumpstart your day off right," said Faith as she entered the bedroom.

"That's great. Thanks. I'll take a drop of cream and two scoops of sugar in mine please."

"Okay, coming right up!" she responded then placed her hand on Kevin's shoulder, leaning in for a kiss. He sat on the bench at the foot of the bed with one leg propped up across the other leg for the convenience of putting on his navy-blue loafers that matched his navy blue and white button up polo shirt.

Faith exited the room and headed towards the kitchen humming a melody when her phone began to ring, interrupting the Pandora tunes that she was reciting.

"Hey Mya" Faith greeted. "How's it going?"

"I've been meaning to call you to see how did attending your multiple events turned out last week?"

"Everything went well. I had a great time, especially pulling off the wardrobe and my fabulous haircut, compliments to you of course!"

"So, I was checking to see if you were with a client right now?" Mya asked.

"No girl, I'm actually client-free right now. Is everything good?" she responded.

"I have Melissa, Jahel and Denise on the line.

Melissa has something she wants to tell us and I wanted to make sure you weren't occupied."

"I'm good," Faith said, as she stepped out onto the balcony for a little privacy.

There was a click in the line and now the call was filled with the sounds of multiple voices. Melissa began to speak, "Hey ladies, how are you all?" she asked. "It's been a long time and I miss you all!"

"We miss you too Hun!" They responded.

"So, I got some news to share that's going to shock the hell out of you, and I wanted to be sure that everyone was able to hear it all at the same time." Before Melissa could proceed with her next sentence Denise blurted out, "Girl you pregnant?"

"Really, Denise," said Jahel.

"What? I'm just asking!" she said, defensively. "I thought she might be the first in the crew to give us a niece or nephew."

"Well, in that case, are you?" asked Faith curiously.

"Come on guys; let Melissa have the floor to share the news that we all are dying to hear," Mya implored. The line went quiet, and Melissa continued on with the conversation as before.

"So, for starters, I'm not pregnant, thank God! But the news is I'm getting married!" shouted Melissa, screaming with excitement.

"O.M.G! Congratulations girl!"

"Okay… Mrs… congrats, I'm so happy for you!"

"This is going to be epic! So have you guys set a date yet?" asked Mya.

"Well, we haven't set an exact date yet, but we're looking to have the wedding ceremony in the month of May."

"Wow, that's like five months away!" said Faith.

"I know right!" replied Melissa. "Looks like I have a lot of planning to do! Don't worry girl, that's why we're here. We'll help you through this process every step of the way," said Jahel. "I'm really going to enjoy this. I didn't get to have a traditional wedding. I got hitched at the courthouse" she stated with a slight giggle at the end of her sentence.

"That's right we're here for you lady," agreed Denise.

"Thanks ladies," said Melissa.

"That's great to hear. Since my parents weren't lucky enough to bless me with sisters, it would be an honor to have you ladies, correction I mean my sisters as my bridesmaids!"

The women all squealed with joy in acceptance of Melissa's bridesmaids' invitation.

"Okay great," Melissa said happily.

"I will be scheduling a weekend at the end of next month to host a pre-wedding party extravaganza. Everyone who is a part of the wedding will be in attendance. During that weekend we will have a fun-filled day selecting our dresses, a meet and greet dinner, wedding dinner party and also enjoy the tea party themed bridal shower."

"Okay, that's different. Sounds elegant and bougie!" said Jahel.

Yeah it was Jacqueline's idea. She insisted that she host the event in addition to her paying for it as well. So, I let her have her way with it," Melissa said. Okay for the mother-in-law!" Faith shouted. "I know right Melissa agreed trying to mask the irritation in her voice.

"Hey I'm down with being prissy for a day!" Denise said in an overly proper tone.

"Well, definitely save that energy for next month because I can't wait to see all of you!" replied Melissa. The ladies expressed their congrats again before they exchanged good-byes and ended their call. After hanging up the phone, Faith realized that she had been on the call for quite some time. She turned around to make her way back to the kitchen when she was instantly startled by Kevin who was standing in the entrance. He slid the door open allowing her to step inside.

"I was starting to get worried about you and my coffee. After ten minutes had passed there was still no sign of you or the coffee," he said teasingly.

"Sounds like you were more concerned about your coffee than me," Faith said as she wrapped her hands around his waist, stood on her tiptoes and planted a soothing kiss on his lips to initiate a silent apology.

"I don't want to seem like I was eavesdropping on your conversation, but I overheard a lot of laughter, joy and excitement."

"Did you get some good news?" he said with curiosity.

"Actually, the good news belongs to my friend. She just got engaged." said Faith as she reached up to grab a mug from the cabinet.

She continued talking as she began adding the condiments to the mug before pouring the steamy hot coffee from the pot inside it. "One drop of cream and two scoops of sugar as you requested," she said while extending her arm out to hand Kevin his personalized cup of coffee.

"By the way, my client texted this morning to let me know that she'll be running about an hour behind for her appointment, so I can give you a ride to the airport and save you the trouble of having to deal with a crazy Uber driver if you like?" Asked Faith.

"You don't have to ask me twice," he replied as he took a sip of his coffee. "After your episode with that last Uber driver, I didn't think you'd decline," she said giggling.

***

The ETA on the GPS map read five minutes before they would arrive at the airport.

"So how long will it be before you come back?" Faith asked Kevin as she merged into the right lane to follow the signs for departures.

"Oh, I should be back in about two weeks," he responded.

"Ugh!" she said, rolling her eyes in the back of her head. "Two weeks seems like such a long time. I miss you so much when you're gone. These business trips are becoming more frequent and the time frames of you being gone are stretching out for longer periods now as well."

"I know honey. The company is really growing at an accelerated rate, but once things get settled, I'll be available to give you all of my undivided attention with no interruptions. Just try to be a little more patient with me and trust the process," he said, placing his hand on top of hers, intertwining their fingers together to provide her feelings and emotions with some reassurance.

"You have arrived at your destination," the GPS alerted as they pulled up to terminal three.

Faith parked the car and popped open the trunk for Kevin to retrieve his luggage. She got out and met him at the rear end of the vehicle.

"I love you. See you soon!" he said, giving her a kiss before walking through the entrance doors of the airport.

CHAPTER TWELVE

The Trip

Mya finally arrived at the airport. She had exactly one hour and fifteen minutes to get her luggage and secured case checked in, which contained very sensitive items that were restricted from being on the airplane as a carry on. She quickly exited her Uber Black as the driver opened her back door. She grabbed her things and made her way through the double glass door. She walked at a swift pace through the radar detector, making a slight turn to the right. Her eyes widened as she noticed the long line of passengers. They were paired in twos, but it would still come out to roughly twenty-five check-ins before she could reach the counter. She sighed in disbelief that there were just as many people who rushed to the airport at the last minute like herself.

Suddenly, a man dressed in navy blue slacks, a white button-up shirt, red necktie and a navy-blue blazer that read American Airlines appeared in front of her. She was so glad she came across an employee at the airport. God was definitely looking out for her.

"You look rather frustrated. Can I help you with something?" He said with a concerned smile.

She pouted at him with a distressed look on her face. You could almost see the twords on her face that screamed, "rescue me please". He could not have come at a better time! She paused for a brief second trying her best to look even more pitiful.

"Yes indeed!" she answered.

After She explained her situation to him, he directed her to an empty counter containing only a computer monitor and a keyboard. He collected her information, tagged her bags, and then handed her a boarding pass, concluding their conversation.

"I hope you have a safe, wonderful trip." he said with a kind smile.

"You are a lifesaver. Thank you so much," Mya said in return, quickly gathering her things and making her way towards gate L19.

Once seated, she leaned back in her chair, comfortably closing her eyes as her body melted like butter on the seat. This was the perfect moment for her to clear her mind for a few hours. She had a long weekend ahead of her and was determined to take advantage of her time.

Mya was awakened by the sound of a male's voice, which she soon recognized as the same voice from earlier before the plane took off. It was the pilot's voice announcing that they had now safely landed in Dallas at 3:45 a.m. She wiped her face with her hands before she rose from her seat, grabbed her carry-on bag from the overhead compartment and made her way down the aisle towards the exit. She followed the rest of the passengers to the luggage pickup station at terminal three.

After watching the conveyor belt filled with a variety of luggage go around for the third time, she finally identified her black and white polka dot suitcase coming in her direction. She scooped it up as she struggled to get it over the lever before both she and the suitcase took an embarrassing and involuntary trip around the conveyor belt against their free will. Afterwards, she secured her 2023 Chevy Malibu rental car, on a mission to find the nearest Coffee Cafe.

Mya pulled into the parking lot on Kirby Dr. She could tell that she was rather early for her caffeine fix seeing that there was not a single car in the lot besides a small yellow Beetle parked near the garbage cans that sat alongside the gate in the back of the parking lot.

She glanced at the blocked formatted numbers on the clock radio to realize that she actually was too early for her mocha Frappuccino. She could almost feel the rush of expectation that the caffeine would give her. She could picture it flowing through her body and she still had at least fifteen more minutes before the coffee shop would even open.

She sighed, reaching into her bag and pulled out her daily planner, quickly flipping the pages to her to-do-list where she had written in the note section at the back of the book. As she went down her list, there was one bullet point that stood out. It was the task of sending off a box filled with the rest of Gibson's items that he failed to collect during the time of their agreement to separate based on their unsettled issues. As her eyes zoomed in and focused deeper on the task her mind began to wonder about recapturing moments that they shared together. There were moments filled with laughter and joy. There were glimpses filled with anger and tears. She snapped back into reality when she recognized that the lights in the cafe were now on.

She pulled up to the drive thru speaker box and began to place her order. Before she eased forward to the pick-up window, she took a quick look in the mirror over the sun visor, being sure to rid her eyes of any unwanted mascara and eyeliner that might have gotten under the bottom of her eyelids as a few tears dropped from her eyes.

The cashier came to the window and greeted her with a delightful smile. "Good morning" She greeted as she repeated her order, announcing the total.

She reached into her purse, took out her wallet, handing her a Visa card. The cashier in return handed over her caffeine in a cup, a slice of lemon cake and a receipt attached to her card. "Have a Happy Friday and a great weekend," she said.

Mya replayed those words in her head as she reached over and closed her daily planner, displaying her to-do-list on the passenger seat. She vowed to herself that she was going to have a great weekend. She was finally back in her hometown, which was a visit that was three years overdue. Her busy life back in New York had put limitations on her availability to travel back home.

She sipped on her caffeine as she entered the information in the GPS for directions to her hotel. After checking in at the front desk, she took the elevator up to the seventh floor and followed the signs for room 716.

She took the key card from the paper sleeve and unlocked the door. The ambiance was just as she expected from the Hilton Suites; nice, elegant and cozy. She made her way to the recliner to catch a short nap. She had about three hours to rest before she would have to shower, get dressed and head over to Melissa's house to meet her for their 10:00 a.m. appointment at the bridal shop.

CHAPTER THIRTEEN

The Reunion

It couldn't have been a better day. The sun was shining and the breeze was calm as it drifted the smell of morning dew through the bedroom window. Melissa was prepared for a fun-filled weekend spent with family, friends and her soon-to-be-in-laws. This was going to be their first official meeting since the engagement party back on New Year's Eve when Stephen proposed to her for the second time.

This came about after he was feeling regrets for proposing to Melissa on Christmas Eve at their favorite restaurant where they went for dinner on their first anniversary of their relationship three years ago. Although the moment was so beautiful, emotional, and special all at the same time, it was like something she'd never imagined. Being the great son he was, Stephen felt he owed it to his mother to fulfill his promise and make sure she was a witness to his marriage proposal. Stephen and his mother had a really close bond. He had always been by her side since his dad abandoned the family for his mistress.

She was the woman he had met while traveling from city-to-city, working for companies around the country as an architect. What made matters worse was the fact that his dad decided to leave two weeks after Jacqueline's cancer was in recurrence. Stephen had promised Melissa that night that he would love, honor and cherish their unity and that he would be a better man to her than his father had been to his mother. She could still feel the passion in those words as she recaptured the moment.

Melissa stared into the mirror while gently running her finger through her hair with a little hair cream to tame any fizziness that may have occurred during her sleep last night.. The corner of her right eye caught a glimpse of a sparkle from her ring though the reflection in the mirror. She smiled as she admired the beauty of her two carat, colorless princess cut diamond, 14 carat white gold ring. It looked great on her finger. The doorbell rang abruptly as she quickly snapped out of her dazed moment.

"Is it after 9 a.m. already?" Melissa exclaimed in shock.

She ran down the stairs excitedly towards the front door, slightly out of breath. From the bottom step, she could see directly through the glass door that it was Mya. She could tell it was her from the side of her face as she stood in a diagonal position from her view. Melissa grabbed the knob and opened the door screaming with joy as she launched forward putting her best friend of 22 years in a lovable bear hug.

Mya laughed hysterically as if someone was tickling her. Melissa took a step back to take a good look at her. It had been three years since they had last seen each other. After sharing warm welcomes, Melissa and Mya took a moment to decide if they were going to drive her car or take Mya's rental car. Since the rental was the last car in line parked in the driveway, they both agreed that it would be simpler to just take the rental.

"So, what's the plan for meeting up with the other ladies today?" Mya asked, breaking the silence.

Melissa paused for a brief second, deep in thought.

"Well, Faith came into town early yesterday morning to provide hair services for a few of my family members and friends that will be attending the dinner party tonight. She'll be taking an Uber to meet us at the bridal shop."

"Would that appointment list happen to include my Aunt Erma?" Mya asked in a joking tone.

"Yess!" Be very optimistic," said Melissa.

Aunt Erma seemed to be the only person in the world who insisted on wearing finger waved hairdos to every occasion she attended and Faith was just that stylist to get her whipped or as Aunt Erma would say "Styling and Profiling!"

After a few giggles, Melissa continued on, "Jahel and Denise will carpool over to the location together. This is going to be the first time in three years since we all have been together. The last time we were together was on our final night in graduate school. We spent our last night in the apartment we shared eating take-out, drinking wine and finishing up the last of our packing.

Instead of packing, we spent the majority of the night laughing and making continuous toasts to memories of our past years together– the good, bad, and the ugly. It's going to be so great to have the whole crew back together again," Melissa exclaimed.

Mya made a right turn into the parking lot of the bridal shop and pulled in the first open space available. She turned to Melissa in question. "So, are you ready to pick out the most important dress you'll ever wear in your lifetime?"

Before Melissa could answer the question, the ladies were interrupted by a tapping sound on the window. To the left was Jahel and to the right was Denise both giving a waving signal for them to exit the vehicle. Before anyone could get a chance to properly greet each other, a car entered the lot and stopped directly in front of them and out jumped Faith.

"Perfect timing" said the ladies in unison, joining arms into one big group hug. Once the hug was released, the ladies giggled with joy as they turned to walk towards the door of the bridal shop. As they entered the shop there was a light sound of a woman's voice that came from an intercom speaker.

"Good morning, ladies. Please make yourselves comfortable and an associate will be with you shortly."

They all looked at each other with grins on their faces as they admired the delightful ambiance. The sound of someone entering the room drew the ladies attention to the glass door as it opened. They were approached by a slender woman wearing a nicely tailored charcoal gray pencil skirt with a matching fitted blazer. She had auburn hair with a well critiqued shoulder length blunt cut that flowed freely as she leaned forward to greet Melissa with a warm handshake.

"I assume you're the bride to be?"

"Yes," Melissa responded with a cheerful smile looking at her friends with a surprised expression, wondering how she knew she was the one getting married. Then she remembered that Jacqueline was the one who selected the bridal shop. *She probably gave them a photo knowing her– being the extra person she is!* Melissa thought.

"I'm Sarah, and I will be assisting you and your guest today to find the perfect dresses to fit your special occasion."

They all smiled as they were led through the glass doors and down the hallway until they arrived at a white door with a sign on it that read "Welcome Bride-To-Be" in gold glitter letters with different shades of pink flowers outlining the border.

When the door opened, the women were all amazed by the elegance of the room. Inside were two luxurious gold tufted leather sofas that sat across from each other. Between the two sat a huge white tufted leather armchair that stood about six feet tall. In the middle of the floor lay a snow white sheepskin fur rug with a glass table trimmed in gold placed on top of it. On the table were two gold platters.

One platter had a bottle of champagne and five flute glasses and on the other platter were a variety of fruits, meats, cheeses, and crackers. The room was filled with different shades of pink flowers that resembled the sign on the door. In the corner of the room was a handcrafted folding room divider and next to it was a clothing rack filled with glamorous dresses for the ladies to choose from.

Melissa took a seat in a huge chair fit for a queen as their assistant Sarah popped open the bottle of champagne and poured a glass for everyone. The ladies all grabbed one as Melissa lifted her glass in a toast and said, "may the best dress win!" The ladies repeated it together as their glasses connected.

CHAPTER FOURTEEN

Tea Party Bridal Shower

66So, are you ready for the tea party?" Denise asked Jahel as she placed her hands that were covered with white lace gloves on top of her white hat covered with several shades of pink flowers. Denise then crossed her legs and began to spin around slowly giving a 360 display of her form fitting strapless pastel pink dress that gave her cleavage a full and plumped look with a slight flare that flowed as she turned around.

"I'm as tea-party-ready as I can be," Jahel said with a smile while posing in a curtsy bow. "I see you've done your research on tea party ethics," Denise said, giving her friend an inquiring eye of curiosity.

"Welcome ladies. May I have your names, please?" a woman asked who was standing at the door holding a digital iPad in her hand as they entered the lobby of the banquet hall. After the two gave their names, the woman used her index finger to scroll down on the iPad screen, lifting her head back to them.

"Okay, I've found you both," she said, reaching down to take two envelopes from the stack that were sitting on the round cocktail table next to her. "Here you go," she stated as she handed them each an envelope. "You may proceed through the double doors to your left and have a wonderful time," the woman said as she concluded their short meet and greet.

"Fancy," said Denise, waving her envelope back and forward as she walked alongside Jahel.

"This is amazing" Jahel exclaimed in amazement, as they entered the double doors into a room filled with several tables draped with white linen each topped with their own unique centerpiece. There were eight chairs at each table and in front of each one were various floral designed porcelain tea cups sitting on the top of matching saucers. Next to it each one was a white mesh bag filled with two herbal tea bags and a porcelain stirrer. There were several standing floral arrangements throughout the room that complimented the fine art painting on the wall.

***

Mya reached inside her purse, scrambling for her phone as it began to ring. She pulled the device out and looked at the screen with uncertainty as it rang for the fourth time, determining whether she should answer the call. Mya's finger was half an inch away from pressing the accept button on the screen when she felt a soft tap on her shoulder along with the sound of a woman's voice.

"Is that my little Niecy Pooh?"

Mya turned around as her Aunt Erma stood before

her with open arms and a huge smile. "Chile that is you!" she said as she lunged forward for a big hug. "Three years has felt like forever," said Aunt Erma as she continued to embrace Mya with warmth. She took a few steps back to admire her beautiful niece. "Turn around for me so I can make sure that you're still in one piece."

"Really, Aunt Erma!" Mya exclaimed with a slight smile. Aunt Erma always did a visual examination of her from head to toe and front to back when she hadn't seen her for more than a week, but in this case, it had been more than three years.

"Well, it looks like you're all intact. Shall we grab a bite to eat?" Aunt Erma stated in a British accent as she roped her arm under Mya's arms and walked towards the tables to be seated. Aunt Erma continued talking in her non origin British accent.

"As I recall there are specific etiquettes and standards that are required to be displayed during a tea party." She began to go into details. "For starters, you never start eating until everyone has been served unless you are directed to do so by your host. Refrain from picking up items from the tower with your fingers. If your server is not present, you must use your fork, and your napkin should be folded on a diagonal and placed on your lap…"

Aunt Erma's information session was briefly interrupted by a server who approached them and placed three tier towers on the table; each one filled with savory and sweet snacks. She continued. "The correct order to enjoy these treats would be to eat the finger savory snacks first," she said pointing at the tower with a choice of cucumber rye, curried egg, and salmon and avocado finger sandwiches.

"Your neutrals will be second" she said while pointing at the tower with a selection of double lemon, orange-cranberry, and raspberry scones. Third will be your sweets," she said as she pointed to the last tower on the table that displayed berry tartlets, hazelnut cake, and vanilla macarons. "Well the best part of all the rules is you can eat all three courses using your bare fingers," Aunt Erma said with a giggle as she grabbed one of the miniature sandwiches from her plate and took a bite.

"Mmm, delicious just as I expected, these little treats will make great snacks for later tonight, she said.

"Later tonight?" Mya asked in confusion.

"Yes, later tonight!" Aunt Erma replied, lifting her arm exposing a few small plastic sandwich zip lock bags. Mya burst into laughter before she could even catch herself.

"Aunt Erma put those away before you get us escorted out of here," she said.

"Alright, but taking a few snacks ain't going to hurt anybody. They're just going to throw the leftovers away! Plus after hearing the amount that Melissa's mother-in-law spent on this event, they are lucky we don't take the silverware too," Aunt Erma said as she slid the plastic bags back into her purse.

"Now that's true!" Mya said, pointing towards Aunt Erma as they both laugh.

***

"What type of tea are you drinking?" Denise said to Jahel.

"Um, I think this is some type of honey lemon zinger herbs," Jahel replied, lifting the wrapper for the tea bag from off the table.

"I would sure love to turn it into some type of cocktail, preferably a long island," She added.

"Now I can use one of those right now at this moment because I got a lot on my mind," said Denise. "Well make that two of us who have a lot on their minds!" Jahel added. "You know there is a spirits store right across the street. We can slip out and run over there, come back, spike our tea and no one will even notice our absence," Denise said frantically.

"For some strange reason, I'm considering taking you up on that offer" Jahel agreed, with much disbelief. "So are you thinking of light liquor, dark liquor, or just something to ease your mind?" Denise asked.

"Let's just go while there's guests still coming in," Jahel said, disregarding Denise's previous question.

***

"Greetings ladies," Faith said as she approached the

table and stood in between Mya and Aunt Erma's chair.

"Hello," they both said in return.

"You look lovely Aunt Erma," Faith complimented.

"Well, you can thank yourself for the main attraction!" Aunt Erma said as she gently patted her head on each side showing off her freshly done finger waves styled by none other than Faith.

"So, where's the rest of the click?" Faith asked, as she searched the room.

"I haven't had a chance to see the woman of the hour yet, but as for Jahel and Denise I think I just saw them exiting the banquet hall before I could get a chance to go over and speak."

"This place is so beautiful," said Faith.

"The receptionist at the front recommended that I check out their Garden of Flowers exhibit in the arboretum. She insisted that I see the various unique flowers brought in from all over the world to contribute to the creation of the divine masterpiece."

"It's definitely a sight to see," Aunt Erma added, agreeing with the receptionist's recommendation.

"I'm going to check it out now. I'll chat with you two in a minute," she replied.

Faith walked out onto the balcony which was easily accessible from the doors located in the back of the banquet hall. She placed both hands on the reeling of the balcony, leaned forward and gazed as she captured her first view of the exhibit in the arboretum.

This was the most exquisite arrangement of flowers collaged together into a superb form of artwork. Faith turned around and headed for the stair so she could get a close and personal look at the exhibit. From the top of the staircase, she could see the parking lot where the guest's cars were parked. There was a vehicle that stood out. It was parked with the hazard lights on directly in front of the building. Faith lifted her foot to take another step down the landing, but quickly grabbed the railing as she stumbled on the stairs. She noticed a man step out of the vehicle holding an unidentifiable object in his hand walking towards the entrance of the building.

Faith frantically turned around and made her way back up the stairs through the balcony doors and glided through the banquet hall passing up the table where she once stood talking with Mya and Aunt Erma who looked at each other confusingly wondering why she was in such a rush. As she exited the building through the entrance doors, Faith's smile melted into an instant frown and tears began to fill her eyes. There stood Kevin locking lips with another woman.

"Thanks Hubby," said the woman. "No problem," he responded as he placed his hands on the woman's waist. "I'll see you guys later." He said to the woman, giving her a second kiss on the lips.

Faith was confused by Kevin's phrase until the woman turned around to head back towards the entrance of the building. From the look of the roundness in her belly, Faith could tell that she was between six or seven months pregnant as she walked directly past her through the doors. Faith stood there on the pavement in a puzzled pause as her eyes made contact with Kevin's.

"Wait Faith! I can explain!" Kevin urged, holding his hand up, signaling for her to hear him out.

Faith cut her eyes at him and immediately turned around and walked away.

CHAPTER FIFTEEN

The Disaster

❝Your friends have been absent for quite some time I would say," Aunt Erma said, her eyes searching for Faith. She did not hear any response. "Chile, did you hear me?" Aunt Erma asked.

"Oh, I'm sorry Auntie," said Mya as she raised her head from looking at her vibrating cell phone underneath the table.

"Yes, you are right I'm going to go around and see if I can't run into them" she said.

"Well, I shall be here sipping tea until you return," Aunt Erma said in her British accent, holding up her pinky finger as she took a sip from the tea cup.

"Is everything ok with you chile? You seem a bit jittery?"

"I'm fine, but thanks for asking," Mya responded as she rose from the table and walked away. From a distance, Mya was able to see Faith walking in a swift motion through the lobby of the banquet hall as the main doors of the room opened and new guests entered the room.

Mya hastened her steps as she headed towards the lobby. Before she could get four steps in, she ran directly into a man who was walking across her pathway. Luckily, he was able to catch her fall as she lost her balance.

"Oh my god, I'm so sorry. I did not see you. Thanks for not letting me fall!" Mya said with a sigh of relief, grateful for his quick response to the incident.

"Ms. Damsel in distress we meet again. So where are you rushing off to this time?" asked the man. Mya took another look at the man who seemed to know her and realized that it was Jacob, the pilot who assisted her at the airport when she first flew out to Dallas.

She was unable to decide which look was more appealing, the one he was wearing now or his look in the pilot uniform. Either way, she knew it was definitely a surprise to see him at this moment. Mya walked through the wooden door labeled women and made her way to the sink as she grabbed a few paper towels from the basket that sat on the counter of the sink. She dampened it with water and began to lightly pat her face to remove the perspiration. She placed both hands on the counter and released a huge sigh as her mind rampaged with the thoughts of Aunt Erma's constant need to check up on her and the continuous vibration of her phone. Then, to add more intrigue to the moment, for some strange reason she ran into the handsome pilot from the airport.

A pleasant coincidence, just wrong timing, she thought, as she smiled.

Mya could hear the sound of weeping coming from one of the bathroom stalls after she twisted the knob to shut off the running water.

"Hey, are you okay?" she asked, but no one responded to her question. Mya slowly moved forward in the direction of the stall from which the sound was coming. She gently knocked on the door and asked again. "Hey are you okay?" The door cracked open enough to see Faith sitting fully clothed on the toilet seat with her face cupped in her hands, crying. Mya pushed the door completely open in an eager attempt to console her friend.

"Hey, what's wrong?" she asked.

Faith removed her hands from her face, shouting, "I can't believe I was so stupid."

"Why do you believe that you're stupid? What happened?" Mya asked.

Faith continued to sniffle rapidly as she took the tissue balled up in her right hand and used it to wipe her nose.

"Would you like to go outside to get some air and talk about it?" asked Mya.

Before Faith could respond, they heard the voices of two women laughing mischievously. Mya stuck her head out the stall door to see Jahel and Denise walking in with a large brown-paper bag.

"Where have you two been?" asked Mya as she stared them both up and down.

"Well, if you must know, Mommie Dearest, we ran to the spirits store across the street to grab some real liquor to liven up this snooty tea party!" Denise shot back in a sassy manner as Jahel giggled.

"Why are you peeking from behind that door?" Denise asked. She stepped forward and snatched the door handle to pull it open.

When she saw Faith wiping her bloodshot red eyes, she knew that this was no longer a joking moment.

"Hey, what happened? You good girl?" Denise asked with concern.

Faith disregarded the question and flatly asked, "What kind of liquor did you say you guys picked up from the store?"

"Um, we grabbed some vodka to remain incognito on the smell."

"Sounds fine to me. Let's drink," Faith said as she jumped up from the toilet and headed straight for the liquor.

Jahel and Denise looked at Mya for answers, but she lifted her hands and shrugged her shoulders giving them the signal that she was clueless as well.

***

"Two more hours don't seem like it can come any faster!" Melissa said, looking in the mirror as she exhaled from her nostrils to let out some of the steam that was building up inside. She walked past the stalls to the lounging area with chairs in the back of the bathroom.

"What's this? The cool kids are cutting class, drinking liquor from the bottle?" Melissa complained, feeling left out when she saw all four of her friends struggling to conceal the liquor bottle from her eyes.

"Naw, it's just a class reunion, if you would like to join," Faith slurred, holding up the bottle of Vodka in Melissa's direction.

"I have learned to turn down a lot of things in my life, but liquor is not one of them," Melissa joked as she grabbed the bottle and took a huge swig.

"So, what's eating at you? This is supposed to be your day of celebration!" Mya asked Melissa.

"I wish someone would tell that to my uptight, controlling, bougie-ass soon-to-be mother-in-law" Melissa shouted softly.

"Oh, honey," Jahel said, shaking her head, "you're eventually going to have to stand up for yourself one day and put her in her place, I will say. Take it from someone who's been in those same shoes," she added while raising the bottle for someone else to take a swig.

Mya's phone began vibrating again. She answered without looking at the screen first.

"Hello?" She blurted out in a drunken tone. "Hey, Melissa this is your favorite cousin calling," she yelled, sloppily waving the phone back and forward in the air.

"Oh, shit what time is it? How long have I been gone?" Melissa asked. Mya handed the phone over. The sound of a woman's voice screaming hysterically blared from the phone receiver.

Melissa hung up the phone, stumbling to her feet and shouting, "This is the last straw. Who in the hell does she think she is to send my favorite cousins away? Telling them that they're not appropriately dressed for the tea party! After she done already cut my damn guest list in half to accommodate her own invite list"

"Oh HEELLLL NO!!" Faith shouted, who was already angry and looking for a fight. "No, ma'am. You need to put that bitch in check!"

"Oh, I got some choice words for Miss Cruella today," Melissa shouted as she staggered towards the bathroom door.

"Yeah, I think it's about time. She's definitely doing too much. You're going to have to do it one day; why not get it over before the wedding!" Jahel joined in.

Each friend took turns dousing gasoline on the fire. Melissa stormed out of the bathroom in an angry rage looking for Jacqueline as her entourage followed.

CHAPTER SIXTEEN

Tough Decisions

66Here's your ID back and your visitor's pass. You can use the elevators to your left and take it to the fifth floor," the receptionist sitting at the front desk said to Mya. Once she arrived at her floor, Mya exited the elevator and checked in with a woman at another desk who asked to see her visitor's pass.

She pointed to the right. "Room 536 is the door at the end of the hall, on the left."

"Thanks, and have a nice day," Mya responded before leaving the desk. She walked down the hallway thinking, in disbelief, about the wild, crazy, and out of control evening that had occurred the night before. It was 8 a.m. and she could still feel the side effects of the liquor she had consumed at the bridal shower. Mya knocked on the room door twice and slowly pushed it open.

"Hey lady, how's it going?" She said in a bashful tone. She was apprehensive about Melissa's response. She walked in and placed a vase of flowers on the nightstand next to the hospital bed.

The lighting in the room was dimmed and the shades were closed. Melissa twisted her head from the window towards Mya.

"Do I look like I'm okay?"

She could tell from the look on Melissa's face that

she was definitely upset, but her words were slurred from the medication she was on. Mya didn't say a word, she simply walked over to the window and opened the blinds to brighten up the room. Melissa sat in an uncomfortable position, slouched down on the bed with her left foot elevated on some pillows.

"For starters, let's get you adjusted properly," Mya said as she approached the bed ready to implement her previous CNA skills she gained as a teenager working with seniors. She stepped behind the bed, reached down and grabbed the folded sheet under Melissa's body pulling it to lift her up in an upright position.

"Now that should feel a lot better, wouldn't you agree?" she stated, Mya continued, not leaving any room for Melissa to reply. "Now let's adjust these foot pillows and you'll be all set," she added as she pulled the covers back and began rearranging the pillows.

Melissa took a sip of water and placed the cup back on the nightstand and began to speak. "The doctor said that I fractured my fibula bone and that I'm going to need to have surgery as soon as possible before my leg starts to heal with a dislocated bone."

"O.M.G., I didn't know it was that bad. I thought that maybe you had just sprained your ankle or something. This is terrible," Mya exclaimed.

"Oh, that's just the beginning of this madness. It gets worse!" Melissa stated as she took another sip of her water and continued to elaborate. "Well after calling the ambulance when I broke my leg, clearly Jacqueline made a call to Stephen to tell him all about the incident. When we made it to the hospital, Stephen was standing at the emergency room door. He just stood there, just staring at me with the look of hurt and disappointment written all over his face." She said sobbing. "Before I could even explain the build up of events that led to what happened with Jacqueline, Stephen said that he refused to marry a woman who gets drunk and disrespects his mother after all she did to make this a special day for me. He called me ungrateful and said that he needed to take some time to reconsider this marriage thing, before we both make a decision we'll end up regretting less than a year from now. He left me here in the hospital all by myself!" Melissa burst into tears as she repeated his words.

Mya stood quietly, still trying to process the information. She sat down on the bed next to Melissa and gently consoled her best friend in this moment of hurt, disappointment and pain.

"I can't believe this is really happening right now!" Melissa wailed.

"If Jahel and Denise hadn't been so immature and inconsiderate enough to bring liquor to my bridal shower, get me drunk, and then hype me up to confront my future mother-in-law, I wouldn't be in this fucked up situation or this damn hospital bed right now. I can just strangle them both! We're not still in college. You know, I can't run around drinking every time an issue comes my way. This will be the last time they'll be able to take part in ruining another event for me. I have decided that they are unofficially my bridesmaids!"

Mya wasn't sure if Melissa was in her right state of mind due to the medication the doctor had given her or if she truly meant those words. Mya sat in silence, her heart filled with empathy for her friend. The doctor came into the room and interrupted the shocking moment that had just occurred.

"So, Ms. Sinclaire, we've got your final x-rays back and it looks like you definitely broke your fibula. Because the injury is on the inner portion of your ankle, we will have to proceed with the surgery as I discussed earlier."

Tears ran down Melissa's face as she sobbed. The doctor placed his hand on her shoulder in pity, a small sense of empathy tugged at his heart. "I'm going to give you some time to digest things before the nurse comes in to explain the logistics of the procedure and get you prepped for surgery. How does that sound?"

"That's fine," she responded in a soft and nonchalant tone. The door closed behind the doctor as he walked out, leaving the room filled with silence.

CHAPTER SEVENTEEN

Overdue Visit

"Hi Aunt Erma," Mya said as she entered the kitchen, removing her jacket and laying it across the chair at the kitchen table. She walked over to the stove where Aunt Erma was standing and gave her a hug from behind placing a kiss on her cheek.

"Mmmm, you got it smelling so good in here," she said as Aunt Erma lifted the lid from the pot and began stirring.

"I thought you could use a warm and comforting meal to soothe your hangover after last night's interesting events," she said.

Mya knew that was Aunt Erma's nice way of saying that last night was a hot mess. "So, I decided to make your favorite, Southern Shrimp Chowder." She grabbed her mittens from the counter, opened the oven, pulled a muffin pan out and sat it on top of the stove. "And to top it off, I also made cheesy corn muffins from scratch using your mom's secret recipe," she added with a smile.

"Looks like I'm in for a treat then," Mya replied without giving any regards to Aunt Erma's statement about her mom's recipe. Aunt Erma reached for two white bowls from the cabinet, filled them with chowder and placed them on the table with a muffin on the side.

"Shall we pray?" she asked rhetorically, extending

her hands out to Mya. "Father God, we come to you today to give thanks for all that you have done for us…"

Mya chuckled inside thinking about how Aunt Erma still began her prayers the same way for as long as she could remember.

"Amen" she said as she ended her prayer.

"How's Melissa doing?" Aunt Erma asked. The warm steam from the soup rose to Mya's face as she took a scoop of the chowder.

"Well, she's pretty upset right now about everything. I stayed at the hospital with her until she was taken away for surgery. The doctor had given her some medication to ease the pain and get her calm before the procedure, and it had her high as a kite!" Mya said laughing. "Melissa was under the impression that her feet were deformed and that she was missing both her big toes. She also refused to let the doctors look at her feet when they tried to remove the sheets because she said they were covered with warts."

"Lord that poor Chile," Aunt Erma said, shaking her head. "I hope all works out for her and her old man, but that mother-in-law of hers is definitely going to have to stay in her own lane for that to happen."

"I agree with you on that," Mya responded.

Mya explained how the big blow up at the bridal shower had resulted in Melissa breaking her leg, Stephen calling off the wedding saying he needed some time to rethink things, and Melissa making them unofficially her bridesmaids.

***

The vibrating sound of her phone woke Mya up from her sleep. She looked at her phone, it was a bit after 6 p.m. and she had notifications indicating that she had missed a few calls. She didn't realize that she had passed out while talking to Aunt Erma on the couch. She instantly checked to see if she had any missed calls from the hospital, there were none. She grabbed her jacket from the kitchen. Aunt Erma came walking down the stairs.

"Chile, from the way you were sleeping, I can tell it's been a long time since you had a good home cooked meal!"

"Yes, I really needed that, it hit the spot," Mya said, stroking her belly.

"I'm going to head back up to the hospital, Melissa should be out of surgery soon. I would hate for her to wake up afterwards alone." She continues, "Oh, and by the way, I'll be working remotely with my job for a couple of weeks, so I'll be able to stay here and help out until she gets back on her feet."

"Oh, that's fantastic!" Aunt Erma exclaimed with her hands pressed together as if she was about to pray.

"So, I can definitely use another one of those home cooked meals again." Mya hinted. "You can have as many home cooked meals as you like Niecy Pooh", replied Aunt Erma.

"Okay I'll call you later," Mya said as she hugged Aunt Erma and walked out of the door.

CHAPTER EIGHTEEN

The Unofficial Bridesmaids

Exactly 6 weeks had passed since Denise had last appeared in front of the judge after being arrested for assault and battery. Although she returned this time prepared with a lawyer, there was still a ball of tension dwelling on her shoulders as she recalled the previous allegations read by the judge against her when she last appeared in court. These were also allegations that she had no recollection of, which made matters worse.

She felt she had no way of defending herself in this situation even if she wanted to because she couldn't remember what actually took place. When it was their turn to go before the judge, her lawyer insisted that she allow him to do all the talking.

"There's no objections on my end" she responded with a sense of relief.

After the lawyer was done making his statement and giving an overall description of Denise as a person, in addition to reading the character letters that had been provided by several colleagues, teachers and friends. The judge decided to go on a brief recess while the prosecuting attorney consulted with her client to decide on their proceeding. The judge suggested that all parties return in two hours.

"I'm going to grab some tea and a bit to eat from the cafe up the street. Would you like anything?" Denise asked her lawyer.

"No thanks, but thanks for asking."

"Ok meet you back here shortly," she said as she walked away.

The waitress walked up to the table with a black circle tray in her hand. She removed the items from it and placed them on the table. "Is there anything else I can get for you at this time?" She asked.

"No thank you. This will be fine for now," Denise replied as she looked down at the mug filled with hot water and a tea bag thinking to herself how she would usually be ordering a lemon drop or some other sort of martini during this hour of the day.

"I thought that was you. I recognized you as I walked past the window. What are you doing here?" Crystal asked as she pulled out the chair and made herself a guest at the two-seat table with Denise.

"The judge gave us a two-hour recess, so I came here to kill some time," Denise said, lifting up her mug filled with hot tea.

"So, how's everything going with that?" Crystal questioned.

"That will be determined when we return to the courtroom," Denise said with a nervous look in her eyes as she sipped her tea.

"Well let's pray for the best!" Crystal said with confidence as she extended her hands to connect with Denise for a quick prayer.

****

Jahel closed the front door as she entered the house. She let out an exhausted sigh, her eyes rolling to the back of her head. She took off her jacket and hung it on the gold metal hook attached to the white wall then bent down to remove her shoes. She slid into her slippers that were sitting next to the shoe rack and made her way down the hall.

"Honey, is that you?" Tyler said as he heard the sound of footsteps approaching.

"Yes, Babes! It's me," she replied while following the sound of his voice that led her to the bathroom in their bedroom. There stood Tyler with a torch lighter in his hand as he continued lighting the candles positioned around the sink and tub. They both were filled with water and on the top surface laid clouds of bubbles sprinkled with velvet red rose petals.

After the last candle was lit, Tyler turned to Jahel and placed a kiss on her lips. "I thought you could use some relaxation time and a good home cooked meal," he added while slowly stroking her hair as if he was giving her a quick head massage.

"I'm going to finish getting dinner ready and I'll see

you shortly," He said and placed a kiss on her forehead.

Jahel began shedding her garments. The tunes of a-romatherapy music played from the Bluetooth speaker in a soothing melody. She stepped into the tub and sub-merged herself in the warm water hoping to relieve her mind of the cluttered thoughts that lingered surrounding their plans and options to conceive a child.

"Dinner smells great Babes," Jahel said as she hugged Tyler from behind, lying her head on his back with her nose smudged against his shirt.

"You smell delicious yourself," he said with a look of hunger in his eyes. He was ready to devour her at that very moment.

"You like, huh?" Jahel bragged flirtatiously. "It's a new body butter cream I got when I was out of town."

"So, what's for dinner?" she asked.

"I thought I would whip up one of my old specialties tonight," he said as removed the lid from the platter in the middle of the table.

"O.M.G., I can't believe you made your baked chicken with bell peppers and onions!" She sniffed some more. "Wow! Is that jasmine rice infused with Thai?" She asked softly. "This was the first meal you ever cooked for me, which happened to be one of my favorite choices from you. I was definitely in need of a home cooked meal after that relaxing bath. You were right. Thanks Babes, you're the best," Jahel said, puckering her lips towards Tyler for a kiss before he pulled the chair out for her to sit.

"If I remember correctly, we usually will have strawberry cheesecake with whip cream on top after this meal." Jahel suggested as she took another scoop of her food. "Hey, I'm just saying that it sure would be a nice treat," she said, smiling as she batted her eyes at him.

Tyler gave a mischievous growl. "You know just what to do to turn me on," he said in response to her gesture that now had him aroused. "Yes, that would be our choice for dessert tonight," he answered in response to her previous question.

"I think I'm going to have my dessert early," he said, pushing his chair back from the table. He got down on both knees and crawled underneath the table. He put his hands on Jahel's thighs and slowly spread her legs apart allowing her robe to fall to the sides.

He began kissing her inner thighs, making his way up. He placed a soft wet kiss on the lips of her vagina and stroked her clitoris softly with his tongue. Jahel's legs quivered with each stroke. The feeling of Tyler's tongue on her made her hands weak. She dropped her silverware while holding onto the edges of the table like her life depended on it.

She leaned her head back, closing her eyes, her soft moans echoed loudly as she reached her climax.

***

Faith opened her eyes in pain. The pressure that

throbbed at her skull through the temples gave her the feeling of a hangover. She looked at the empty bottle of wine toppled over next to her as if it was her companion last night. She slowly scooted towards the edge of the bed, reaching for her purse that was on the floor.

She pulled the cellular device out and stared at it for a moment trying to determine if she was ready to turn it back on. Faith realized that it had been powered off for three days now and figured that people would begin to get worried about her sudden disappearance. She held the power button down for a few seconds then released it.

"Fuck! It's dead!" she shouted as she slammed the phone against the bed. She then took her hand on another tour through her purse and located the charger she used to plug up the phone. Faith made her way to the bathroom to rejuvenate herself. She smelled horrible after spending the last few days in the bed, drinking wine. She stepped into the steamy shower as the water sprayed her body with tiny droplets of warm goodness. She placed her head under the running water allowing it to penetrate her, giving her a soothing and warm touch.

She crossed her arms around her body and squeezed herself tightly as she burst into tears. Her back pressed against the glass doors as she slid down to the floor of the shower. She continued crying as the image of Kevin with that pregnant woman tormented her mind. It was the ultimate betrayal.

After the hot water streaming from the shower head

began to turn cold, Faith forced herself to get out of the shower. She stroked her head back and forth with a towel to dry her hair as she stood in her black silk robe looking down at her phone lying on the bed. She figured before she decided to turn it back on to reconnect with the world, she would prepare herself first. She quickly made her way to the bar area to grab a bottle from the wine cooler and a glass from the top shelf.

Faith returned to the room, flopped down on the mattress and poured herself a full glass of wine, took a big gulp, and pressed the power button. Once the phone was fully restarted, she immediately received a notification showing over a hundred voicemails. She braced herself for a moment, hitting the option that allowed her to hear the messages.

"Hey Lady, just calling to check your availability, I need a hair appointment ASAP. Call me back!"

The next message was from Mya, "Hey girl, I've tried calling you several times, just wanted to check up on you, haven't heard from you since you left Dallas. Hope everything is good. Call me back when you get a chance, love you."

The next set of about 30 messages were all from Kevin. The messages became so repetitive and annoying that Faith began deleting the messages without listening to them instantly the moment she heard his voice.

CHAPTER NINETEEN

The Therapy Appointment

"Okay Missy, I think we are all set to go." Mya said standing in front of Melissa with a pair of crutches in her hand. "I'm going to pull the vehicle up close, so you won't have to walk too far,"

she added before handing over the two metal bars to Melissa that would become an extension of her arms to assist her with getting around.

There was complete silence in the car on their ride to the rehabilitation center. Mya pulled into the lot and was able to instantly grab a parking space that was only a few feet from the entrance door just as another car was backing out. "Perfect timing" she said, breaking the code of silence that had been going on for the entire fifteen minutes of their ride.

"Hey lady, I just wanted to let you know that I appreciate all that you're doing with adjusting your work schedule and taking the time out of your busy life to assist me with my recovery. I don't know what I would have done if you weren't here," Melissa said as her eyes teared up.

Mya could feel the sensation of water begin to build up under her eyelids. "Well I'm glad I can work remotely." She responded. "Plus, it's no problem I could use some time away from both that city and the job," Mya stated, reaching for Melissa's hand to help pull her from the vehicle. Once she was able to sustain her balance, Mya passed her the crutches and they headed towards the entrance of the rehab center.

"So have you had a chance to talk to Stephen yet?" Mya asked.

"I actually spoke with him for the first-time last night since our incident," she responded.

"What did he say!" Mya asked, anticipating her response.

"Well, he was definitely in shock when I told him about my leg. He was also upset because I didn't call to inform him when I first found out. I tried explaining to him how I was upset and embarrassed all at the same time. I mean how could I call on him for sympathy after all that was going on." She insisted.

"Yeah, I definitely understand, but hey I'm also a woman," Mya said, lifting her hands while shrugging her shoulders. "How did the conversation end," she asked.

"To sum it up we agreed to meet next week for our previously scheduled premarital counseling appointment with the pastor and see how things go from there," she replied, shaking her head.

***

"If I didn't know any better, I would say that you're following me from one place to another", Jacob insinuated in a flirtatious manner as he walked up to Mya who was sitting in a chair against the wall in the guest lobby area of the rehab center.

"Well, I guess I can say the same thing" Mya said in her defense with a blushing smile.

"Looks like you're all intact," he said as he examined her with his eyes from head to toe. "So, what brings you here?" He asked.

"Oh, I'm here with my best friend. She recently had surgery due to a fractured fibula bone. And you? What's your reason for being here?" she asked in curiosity.

"Oh, I come to bring my granny here for her appointments when I'm in town," he replied. "Come to think of it, you might know her, I brought her to that event when I bumped into you the last time. She's a close friend of Jacqueline."

"Okay, now that would explain why you were the only man in the vicinity of a bridal shower tea party," Mya chuckled.

"Yes, you would be correct," he said with a smile, exposing his polished white teeth that paired well with his handsome face. "I'll be in town for about two weeks. Would you like to join me for dinner tomorrow evening or do I have to coincidentally bump into you again." He said teasingly.

"I just might make you wait to see," she responded

teasingly as she unlocked her phone, handing it to him to enter his number. The door of the guest lobby room opened, a blonde-haired woman wearing an all-white scrub uniform walked in.

"Ms. Sinclaire is ready now. You can meet her at the front desk," she said.

"Okay thanks," Mya responded. "I have to go. I'll talk to you later." She said.

"I'll be waiting," he answers as she walks away from him, following the woman towards the door trying her hardest to rip the blush from her face.

CHAPTER TWENTY

The Shopping List

ya sat her laptop on the dashboard of the car and opened it with the screen facing in her direction. She pulled the sun visor down to take a quick look in the mirror. She adjusted the collar on her blouse, tucked her hair behind her ears, and applied some gloss to her lips. She took another look at her image reflecting in the mirror.

She glanced over at her purse when she heard the muffled sound of a ringing phone. She lifted the purse up and grabbed her phone from underneath it. She took one look at the number on the screen, hit the do not disturb notification and then dropped it in the cup holder. She closed the sun visor and logged into her zoom video call on the laptop.

"Good morning," she said, greeting her colleagues as their faces appeared in individual squares on the screen.

***

Mya hit the horn twice as Aunt Erma closed the front door and made her way down the stairs to the car. "Chile my apologies for the wait, I was stuck on the phone with one of the members at the church. The committee needed my feedback on an urgent matter that had been discussed in my absence during the last committee meeting," said Aunt Erma.

"That's unusual for you!" said Mya. "Oh, I was unable to attend. I had been under the weather for a few days," she replied. Mya turned her head towards the passenger seat where Aunt Erma was sitting. "I didn't know you were ill. Why didn't you tell me? When was this?" she asked with a concerned expression on her face.

"Oh Chile, that was a few weeks ago. It was just a bug that came and left. I'm all good now, no worries!" Aunt Erma said with a smile as she placed her hand on top of Mya's that rested on the gear shift and gently grasped it to provide her with some reassurance.

***

"Do we need a shopping cart or one of these hand baskets?" Mya asked Aunt Erma.

"I think we'd better go with the shopping cart. I got a nice hefty list of items to retrieve," she said, holding up a sheet of paper with words and numbers written on it. Mya grabbed one of the metal carts and they headed down the produce aisle of the store.

"How's Melissa doing?" asked Aunt Erma as she sorted through the pile of tomatoes giving them a gentle squeeze to determine the firmness.

"She's doing fine. Just going to therapy and taking things one day at a time," responded Mya.

Aunt Erma handed the clear bag filled with tomatoes

to Mya to put in the cart. "How are the other ladies doing?" she asked. Aunt Erma always seems to have a way of getting her questions in.

"Well, I've spoken briefly with Jahel and Denise. They were apologetic about everything that happened. They said Melissa hasn't answered or returned their calls. They also received text messages indicating that they were excluded as bridesmaids in the wedding! I haven't had a chance to speak with Faith. I called her a few times and left messages, but she hasn't responded. I know she was going through something that night of the bridal shower, unfortunately we never got a moment alone to discuss what it was." Mya said tiredly.

"I hope she's alright, and I pray that everything smoothes out with you ladies." Aunt Erma said. "So how have you been yourself?" she asked Mya as she handed her more items to put into the cart.

"You know me; pushing it as usual, basically staying busy," she responded.

Aunt Erma kept the questions coming. "When are you going to take some time out for yourself, to open up your heart and let love in again?" This question took Mya by surprise but before she could respond, the tip of their shopping cart collided with the front end of another cart.

"Mya?" inquired the voice of the man she hit.

"Andre," she shouted, hoping she didn't look too excited by his appearance. Andre was Mya's ex-boyfriend, the first guy to grasp a piece of her heart. What were the odds of her running into him at this specific grocery store not even five seconds after Aunt Erma happened to ask that exact question, she wondered.

"How Ironic!" said Aunt Erma as if she had just read Mya's mind. It had been at least three years since they had last seen each other. And there he was looking like fresh fruit in the produce aisle just as handsome as ever.

"How have you been?" Aunt Erma asked, breaking the awkward silence and Mya's indecent thoughts.

"I've been great. Thanks for asking," he replied, returning the question.

"How have you beautiful ladies been?"

Mya couldn't resist blushing, but no words left her mouth.

"We're doing just fine!" Aunt Erma responded for them both.

"So, Mya, how long have you been in town or how long will you be in town?" Andre asked with curiosity.

Aunt Erma gave Mya a nudge, she instantly snapped back into reality. "Oh, I've been here for about two weeks, and I'll be in town for about another two weeks or so."

"Ok that's good. Hopefully we'll get a chance to hook up for lunch or something while you're here," Andre said with a smile.

Aunt Erma gave Mya another nudge to restart her attention again before she responded to his comment.

"Oh yeah, sure that'll be great," she said.

"Ok cool, I'll let you ladies get back to your shopping," he said then continued down the aisle with his cart.

"Chile, you still are the worst at hiding when you're attracted to a man!" Aunt Erma said.

"Was it that obvious?" Mya asked shyly as she placed her index finger on the corner of her lip, with a slight smile on her face.

Aunt Erma gave her niece a stare before they both burst out in laughter. They both continue on shopping for the items on the list.

***

"Girl you won't believe who I ran into today!" Mya said as her eyes widened in excitement waiting for Melissa to respond. It seemed like they were playing a game.

"O.M.G., who?" Melissa said, but before Mya could respond, she continued with more questions. "Wait, is it male or female?" she asked, searching for clues to help determine her answer.

"Well for starters it's a male," Mya hinted.

"Is this male young or old?" Melissa asked next.

"He would be considered middle aged I guess," Mya said giggling as she watched her friend try to figure out who this individual was. "More clues please!" Melissa demanded in a playful way as she gave Mya a gentle shove. Mya giggled again admiring her friend's eagerness to get more information. She continued, giving Melissa more details. "He's tall, dark, handsome and has the perfect physique."

"Girl you must be talking about Andre because he's the only person that I know who makes your eyes light up like that when you speak of him!" she blurted out as she smirked giving Mya the naughty eyes.

"What?" Mya said with a bashful look on her face. "I couldn't resist seeing him looking like a whole snack at that store today". They both released a laughter indicating that the sight of a fine man can be a distraction; especially a man like Andre.

"Okay, on a serious note, how did it feel seeing him today because it's been about three years now since you've last seen him face to face." Melissa asked in a concerned voice.

"Oh, I was definitely taken by surprise when I laid eyes on him." Melissa sat quietly as Mya provided her with additional details to give her a clear vision of the scene that took place with Andre at the store.

"After seeing him today, I would say that I have had so many memories run across my mind of our past," she said with a smile on her face as if she was daydreaming about one of those memories at this very moment.

"Okay, well I hope you don't forget to remember everything from your past, the good, bad and ugly side of things!" Melissa said bluntly, hoping to not offend Mya with her response.

"I just know you had a hard time getting over him after things fell apart between you both around the time of your mom's..." Melissa paused for a second never finishing her previous sentence and continued. "I know what you went through firsthand and I just don't want to see you in that hurt state again that's all," Melissa said with sincerity in her eyes.

CHAPTER TWENTY ONE

The Set Up Plan

❝Have you ladies had a chance to smooth things out yet?" Aunt Erma asked Mya as she placed a plate of bacon, eggs and two fluffy pancakes drizzled with fresh fruit in front of her.

"To answer your question, no! But I do know if you keep making me good meals like this I just might have to move back home!" Mya said laughing while cutting the pancakes. She placed a slice in her mouth and continued speaking.

"To sum it up, Melissa is still upset and being very stubborn about everything and the other girls are starting to get irritated about the whole situation. It's all a mess right now," she said, stuffing her mouth with more pancakes. I've been trying to talk to them all, but it seems useless at this moment with everyone so moody.

"Chile, you girls are going to have to learn that being angry, bitter, stubborn and holding grudges, ain't gone get you nowhere in life, but only hinders you and puts restraints on your own mental, and physical health, preventing spiritual growth," Aunt Erma counseled as she poured more orange juice in Mya's half-filled glass. She continued preaching, waving her hand in the air and shaking her head. "You gotta live for today. We ain't promised tomorrow."

Mya sat quietly taking in every word that came from her mouth. After going on for quite some time, Aunt Erma brought the conversation to an end with a prayer.

"I'm going to head out now, Aunt Erma! I have to jump on a Zoom meeting for work while I'm on my way to pick up Melissa to take her to her therapy appointment. I really appreciated the breakfast this morning. It made me realize how much I miss and enjoy your cooking!" Mya said, while embracing Aunt Erma with a big hug.

"It was my pleasure Niecy Pooh. There's always a seat at my kitchen table for you." Aunt Erma responded with a smile as she pinched Mya's cheek making her giggle.

"You know you've always been the peacemaker amongst the group. Maybe there's something you can figure out to get those girls back on one accord. You have such a humbling spirit that radiates the energy they need at this time." She added.

"I don't know. I'm not trying to be in the middle. I'm the impartial one right now," Mya said.

"I know, and that puts you in the perfect position because you're able to communicate with everyone." Aunt Erma explained.

"Ok I'll think about it, but I really gotta go now," she said looking at the time on her phone as she headed out the door.

"Okay are you coming by later?" Aunt Erma shouted

to Mya as she walked up the driveway towards her car. Mya turned to face Aunt Erma who was standing on the porch then responded

"Actually I won't be stopping by tonight. I have dinner plans at 7 p.m.."

"Oh, okay, well enjoy. I'll see you tomorrow. Love you." Aunt Erma said.

"Love you too Auntie."

***

"I didn't think you were going to call," Jacob said, looking up at Mya with a curious face. She took a sip of water from the straw in her glass then placed it on the table.

"My apologies for taking so long. I've been so busy with work, spending time bonding with my aunt and taking care of my best friend while she recovers," she informed him.

"Oh, no worries. It only took four days," he teased. "No honestly, I definitely understand and just appreciate you finding some time out of your busy schedule to call. After running into you so many times by coincidence, I felt it was only right to have a chance to get to know you better," he said, revealing a handsome smile.

"Are you all ready to order?" the waitress interrupted asking as she approached their table holding a tiny booklet in one hand and a pen in the other hand. Jacob looked at Mya who gave him the eye signal that she was ready.

"Sure, we're ready," he responded.

"I would like the honey garlic salmon from the chef's choice option," Mya stated as she handed her menu to the waitress.

"You know what; you can make those two honey garlic salmons!" he added, "Also can I see the menu for your wine selections?" he asked.

"Sounds great! I'll be right back with that menu for you Sir," the waitress said and walked away.

By the time their dinner had arrived at the table, they were already one glass in on the wine and very heavily engaged in their conversation. They took turns going back and forward asking each other questions about their lives, careers, hobbies, and future goals. The salmon sizzled in its juices as they laid on the cedar planks in front of them.

"This looks and smells amazing. This was a great choice!" Jacob said, raising his glass to salute her with a compliment on the food selection. "So, how's your friend's recovery coming along with the therapy?" he asked.

"She's getting better by the day," Mya said with certainty. "I just wish I could say the same about everything else," she said as she shook her head and took another drink from her wine glass.

"What do you mean by 'everything else'?" he asked.

With the wine beginning to kick in, Mya became more relaxed and began releasing it all.

"For starters, we all had a mini-side party in the

bathroom during the bridal shower, before we immaturely egged Melissa, who was fueled by liquid courage, to confront her future mother-in-law who she felt was very arrogant and controlling over the entire event. After hearing about the ordeal, Stephen postponed the wedding which is a little over a month away. As you can see, Melissa broke her leg and is stuck wearing a cast boot for six weeks, and to make matters worse, she has removed all her friends as bridesmaids from the wedding including me," she said with a giggle. "Currently, no one is talking with each other because of this whole mess," Mya said, twirling the empty wine glass in her hand.

"Wow, yes that's definitely a lot." Jacob responded to the ear full of dramatic events he'd just heard.

"I know, right! I feel so terrible about the role I played in not defusing the situation before it turned into this disaster. At some point, I should have stepped in," she said.

After the bill was paid, they thanked the waitress and got up from the table. Jacob held the door open for Mya to walk out as they exited the restaurant and made their way to the parking lot.

"I really enjoyed having dinner with you tonight," she said.

"You're welcome. I'm glad you found time in your schedule to call," he responded as they approached her car.

"Since I spent most of the time tonight talking about

me, maybe we can have lunch so I can get a chance to learn more about you," Mya suggested, exposing a smirk filled with curiosity on her face.

"Just let me know the date and time and I'll be there," Jacob said as he grabbed the handle on the car door and pulled it open.

"I hope everything works out with you and your friends. If there's anything I can do to help, just say the words," He stated. There was a brief moment of silence as Mya stood face to face with the handsome gentleman who had taken her attention the entire night. About a hundred naughty thoughts ran across her mind before she snapped back to reality.

"Ok I'll give you a call tomorrow," she said, quickly jumping in the car hoping that he didn't sense her current awkwardness.

"Sounds good," he said as he closed her door and walked away to a black SUV parked across from her vehicle.

CHAPTER TWENTY TWO

Unfinished Business

ya noticed a huge pickup truck with large tires parked in Aunt Erma's driveway as she slowly turned in pulling up as much as she could without leaving the tail of her vehicle hanging in the walkway. She conducted a sly investigation of the fancy truck and the contents inside as she passed it, wondering who could possibly be visiting Aunt Erma at this time of day.

After a few rings of the doorbell and no answer, she began knocking on the door. She grabbed her cell phone from her purse to call Aunt Erma on her house phone. Mya twisted the doorknob to see if it was locked before making her way back down the stairs, growing slightly concerned about her aunts' whereabouts. She went around to the side of the house and walked along the concrete path that led to the backyard where there was no trace of Aunt Erma.

As she was about to turn around to make her way back to the front of the house, she heard a sound that seemed to be coming from the garage. She rushed towards the garage's side door and pushed it open in a panic. To her surprise, inside stood Aunt Erma and Andre who was standing up on a ladder. They both turned and looked in her direction. "Mya, Chile is everything okay?" Aunt Erma asked as she looked at her startled face.

"Yes, Aunt Erma. You just had me worried to death!

I'd been calling your phone all morning and was unable to get you on the line, so I came over to check on you. I got here and saw a truck in the driveway that I didn't recognize and you didn't answer the front door. You had me alarmed and concerned, that's all." Mya said as she held her right hand across her chest before releasing a big sigh of relief.

"I was having trouble with my garage opening and closing so I called Andre to come out and help me get it working properly again. Andre has his own electrical repair company, you know. I was just back here keeping him company while he worked."

Andre stepped down from the ladder. "Yep, I think you're all set now," he said as he handed Aunt Erma the remote to the garage to test it out herself. She clicked the square button on the fob as the steel door gently lowered until it was completely closed.

"Yeah, we're all set now. How much is my tab?" asked Aunt Erma.

"This one's on the house!" Andre replied as he pulled out a few cards from his wallet and gave them to her.

"Just remember to tell a friend."

"You've always been so generous," she responded with a delightful smile on her face. "I will surely spread the word to the ladies at Bingo on Monday nights. They can definitely use a helping hand. Most of them are retired, divorced or widows," she added.

"Ok, sounds good. I'll get this stuff cleaned up and let you get on with your day!" He said while pointing to the materials on the floor used for his project. After he was done, Andre approached the front porch as Aunt Erma and Mya sat on the stairs chatting with one another.

"Ok ladies, everything is all cleaned up. I'll be heading out," he said.

"Thanks for taking care of Aunt Erma's garage door today, I really appreciate it," Mya said in an innocent and flirtatious voice. She leaned forward with her elbow on her knee, placing her fist underneath her chin as a prop to hold her head up.

"You're welcome," he replied.

"I'm actually about to grab some lunch before I head back to work if you'd like to join me?" asked Andre. Mya instantly looked at Aunt Erma.

"Oh Chile, no need to worry about me. It's my afternoon nap time" she responded as she waved her hands in the air giving Mya the signal to accept the lunch offer.

"Umm ok, but I need to stop by my hotel first. I forgot my laptop earlier and I have some very important documents that need to be emailed to a client before 2 p.m.." Mya said as she glanced at her watch which read 12:39 p.m. "If you like, there's a restaurant located downstairs in the hotel I've been wanting to check out. It will only take five minutes to send the email," she added.

"Sounds good to me!" Andre said.

"Enjoy!" said Aunt Erma, waving as they left.

***

Mya and Andre's lunch date became happy hour time as they began ordering rounds of drinks. As the drinks flowed, the two reminisced about their past shenanigans and experiences as adolescence, teenagers, and young adults. Laughter bellowed from their table, reminding them both of how long they've known each other.

"Excuse me. We will be shutting down the dining area in about thirty minutes to prepare for dinner." said the waitress who had been assisting them during lunch. "If you like, I can close out your tab here then get you all a table in the pool area? You will still be able to order drinks, appetizers and some of the selected entrees from our full menu."

Mya shrugged her shoulders and looked at Andre trying not to seem too eager to remain in his company while secretly hoping he would play hookie from work and stay.

"Yes, that would be great," he answered as he handed her his credit card to take care of the check without even looking at the bill first. Mya's heart leaped with joy.

"I thought you had to go back to work?" Mya asked him once the waitress walked away.

"Well that's the joy of being your own boss!" He responded.

"Okay, then. If you're going to skip work, let me do the same and take my laptop upstairs so I won't get tempted to check my emails," she said with a giggle.

"Yes, please drop it off. I see you're still a workaholic," he interjected with a smile.

The sound of the elevator dinged as the doors opened. Mya and Andre both excited, laughing and joking, somewhat nervously to room 322. Mya slid her key card and twisted the silver handle. She noticed her hand shaking.

"I'm going to put this laptop away and change into some slides really quick. I might want to get my feet wet!" she said with a smile as she opened the room door.

"I feel you," Andre said in response to her comment while looking down at the sneakers on his feet. "Is it okay if I use your restroom while you change your shoes?" He asked.

"Of course!" She said pointing to the restroom door. Mya walked over to the closet grabbing both handles on the double doors and pulled them open. She scanned the floor for a pair of flip flops or slide-ins that would be suitable for the pool area but she had left them at Melissa's house for the days she spent assisting her. She only had her brown leather strapped sandals.

She heard the sound of running water coming from the bathroom indicating that Andre was finishing up. The bathroom door opened as soon as she took a seat on the softly cushioned velvet blue bench and began removing her shoes to put on the sandals.

"Let me help you with that," Andre offered as he

waited for a signal of approval. She silently responded with a smile, handing him the shoe in her hand. Mya watched closely as he crouched down in front of her, holding her foot and placed it on his knee as he slipped on the sandal and adjusted the strap around the ankle.

"Thank you," she said in a sweet flirtatious tone as Andre released her leg and reached for her hands and pulled her up from her current sitting position. They were standing in close proximity to each other, the mixture of their fragrances combined into a delightful smell that filled the space.

"We should be heading back down to the bar in the pool area. I think I'm due for another drink," Mya said as she exhaled, releasing her breath.

"Yes, I can agree with that," he replied to her suggestion as they regrouped and began to walk towards the door.

Their scents intertwined, following them as they walked through the room. Andre's hand connected with Mya as he leaned forward to intercept her and grab the door handle. The warm touch of his hand alarmed her with a sensation. Her eyes went from looking down at their hands to focusing on his face, his eyes, his lips.

"I miss the beautiful person you are," he said, raising her hand to his lips, placing a kiss on it. "I miss your beautiful smile too," he said, placing a kiss on her cheek. "I miss the taste of your sweet lips the most," he said next as he took his index finger using it to lift her chin and placed a kiss on her lips.

He began kissing her on the neck as he ran his fingers down the middle of her breast making his way south to the waist of her jeans and unbuckled them. Mya let out a slight moan as his kisses got more intense. She gripped the back of his head with her hands trying to resist the feeling, but Andre continued on with his assignment ensuring that no spot went untouched by his lips.

He had her pantless and planted up against the wall in a sleeveless onesie. He placed another kiss on her lips before he bent down on his knees, placed her right leg up on his shoulder, unsnapped the onesies and began softly stroking her pearl tongue with the tip of his tongue. She closed her eyes allowing her head to fall back against the wall, moaning while biting on her bottom lip.

She could feel the exquisite structure of his muscular tone as she gripped his shoulders then began running her fingers down his back. She quickly tightened her grip around his frame as she felt her leg that was positioned on the floor rise as if she was floating away. Andre carried her through the room, gently laying her half-clothed body down on her back stretch across the bed. He stared at her seductively as he took both his index and middle fingers and slowly ran the tips of them past her lips continuing to drift between her breasts.

Once he arrived at her navel, he stopped and looked up at Mya again, this time looking for a sign of approval. He could see that look in her eyes silently screaming "I approve." He slowly spread her legs apart and dove in headfirst to service her for a second time. She used one of her free legs and began to stroke it back and forward against the crouch of his pants, getting him aroused even more as she felt the firmness of his erection.

Andre rose up directly in front of Mya, grabbed her by the leg that had been providing a sensual feel on him, and flipped her over on her stomach. He placed both his hands around her waist and pulled her body up till she was positioned on all fours. He massaged her hips as he gripped them in the palm of his hands. His right hand gently pressed down on the middle of her back propping her ass up in a tilted direction towards the ceiling.

The sound of his unbuckling belt and zipper drove Mya mad with sexual anticipation. She moaned in ecstasy as he slid his dick into her tunnel, and he replied in kind after feeling the warm and wet sensation of her pussy. His eyes closed as he savored every stroke while gaining a tighter grip on her waist. He exploded on her back as his body jerked back and forth in pleasure.

Mya couldn't believe what had just happened so quickly in a matter of minutes of being alone with Andre. She decided to disregard her inner thoughts and just enjoy the moment for all it was worth. Besides, the release was much needed.

CHAPTER TWENTY THREE

Planning the Trip

"So, how's the plan to get your crew back together going?" Jacob asked as they sat at the cafe table sipping their soothing hot chai tea lattes. Mya paused for a second placing her index finger on her cheek.

"Well, I've been giving it some thought, and I was thinking about planning a girls trip where we can all relax while trying to sort out our differences regarding this whole fiasco," she finished before taking another sip from her teacup.

"Okay that sounds interesting, but I'm just wondering with all the confusion going on, how do you plan to get everyone to one destination with no arguments or complaints?" Jacob inquired.

"Great question!" Mya replied before she began to elaborate on the plan she had been concocting in efforts of getting the girls all back together. "I'm still trying to figure out how to mend the relationship between Melissa, Jacqueline, and Stephen, I don't know how or where to begin with that issue!" She added as she raised both her hands halfway bent in the air while shrugging her shoulders indicating that she had no strategic plan in place for resolving this matter. Mya continued sharing some perspective ideas as to how she was planning to pull this all off while Jacob sat quietly listening.

Mya leaned her head to the side as it pressed up against her hand on the table. She released a huge sigh filled with distress. "Don't worry too much, it will all work out somehow." Jacob said as he placed his hand on her shoulder reassuring her that everything would be okay.

A smile appeared on her face as the touch from his hand ignited a warm sense of comfort flowing through her body. "Thanks for being a listening ear," she said as she placed her free hand on top of his. There was a brief moment of silence before it was broken by the releasing of their hands.

"No problem, I might have a few ideas that may be helpful to resolve some of your madness. Give me a day or two to work on some things and I might have a solution for you." He said to Mya as he took the last sip of his latte, took out his wallet and placed a few crispy green bills on the table to cover the tab.

"I need to head over to the clinic to pick up my grandmother from therapy, so I'll chat with you later," he stated before gently grabbing her hand and placing a soft kiss on it. She looked up at him with a bashful smile, trying not to bring too much attention to the way that kiss sent butterflies through her stomach.

"Okay," she responded. As Jacob walked away from the table, Mya sat pondering in thought as to how he was possibly going to be able to help her resolve this tangled situation.

***

"At this time, we would like to ask everyone to fasten their seatbelts as we prepare for landing in approximately 20 minutes," said the captain over the intercom as a female flight attendant walked down the aisle collecting trash.

Mya sat back in her chair thinking about how the vibe would be once her friends realized that they had all been tricked. Mya invited the girls separately to Miami, claiming she was being honored at an event hosted by her company and she needed a guest to join her. She told each of them it was a last minute thing and no one else was available to join her. They had no idea what they were in for. They were under the impression that the job would be presenting her with the "Golden Star" award for being the top ranked marketing consultant of the firm for the last three years. It was a title that had never been received by a female. Mya giggled to herself as she envisioned the expressions on her friends faces when everything unfolded.

"Yep, they're going to kill me!" She silently thought, while nodding her head back and forth as if she was approving of her own answer. Although it was unlike Mya to lie to her friends, she knew at this point she would have to get out of character and use a little manipulation to activate this plan.

There was no way she was going to let this madness

continue to interrupt their sisterhood. Mya had no siblings. Her friends were the next best thing to having some and she valued their relationship too much to see it go down the drain.

Mya's heart warmed as she thought about Jacob and his help with planning and executing this plan. She couldn't believe how, in such a short period of time, she'd unexpectedly met such a handsome gentleman as him and built a connection so quickly. She was worried that the imperfections and drama had to be coming soon. This relationship seemed too good to be true.

CHAPTER TWENTY FOUR

The Meet Up

❝Okay Ms. Green, I see here you have a reservation for five!" The man said standing behind the black hostess booth as he looked up from the computer screen. "You're a little early for your reservation, but if you like I can get you seated at your table or you're welcome to wait at the bar until your party arrives." Mya desperately felt the need to have a drink before the other ladies arrived, but just not at the bar.

"I would like to be seated at our table and you can get me started with a shot of tequila and a margarita on the rocks please!" Mya said as the hostess led her to a secluded section in the back of the restaurant that wasn't too far away but not too close to where the other patrons were seated. The spot was perfect.

There was a circle table with five chairs placed around it, allowing everyone to be on the same level and able to make eye contact during conversation. Mya purposely intended to show up early to give herself time to get comfortable with the atmosphere and prepare herself for what was yet to come. The waiter sat a napkin on the table and placed the drinks she requested on top of it. "Is there anything else I can get for you at this time?" The waiter asked.

"No thank you," she responded. He nodded his head

and walked away.

"Here's to always trying to make the best of things!" Mya said for a little encouragement as she grabbed the shot glass from the table, lifting it up to salute herself before tilting her head and throwing the drink down her throat. Her face scrunched up as if she had just sucked the juice from a lemon. Next, she picked up the margarita and took a sip as she patiently awaited the arrival of her friends.

"Okay Mya what's going on? Because I see your plus one invite has turned into a plus four!" Melissa said as she looked around, cutting her eyes at the other women sitting at the table wondering what reason could they possibly have for being here.

"Okay just give me a minute to explain everything" Mya quickly responded, slightly raising her hands gesturing as she pressed downward signaling for everyone to remain calm once she saw a shift in the scowling facial expressions of the ladies sitting at the table.

Mya began to express her concerns for their friendship while revisiting the episodes that took place at the bridal shower. Mya took the initiative to take accountability for the role she played in egging Melissa on to confront Jacqueline and check her about her behavior.

"I admit, I have not been in a good space lately. I haven't been fully open and honest with you all about my past relationship with Gibson and how we broke up. He was extremely violent and had been for quite some time."

Tears ran down her face as she quickly grabbed the

napkin from underneath her glass to pat her eyes. The table was silent. The women were speechless, blank looks were on their faces as they sat in disbelief. They could not have been hearing the words that were coming out of her mouth correctly.

Faith's eyes watered as she sat next to Mya at the table. She reached over and placed her hand on top of Mya's, providing them both with comfort as she broke the awkward silence at the table.

"We never really got around to talking about why I was crying in the bathroom stall the night of the bridal shower."

They all waited in anticipation.

"Well, truth be told!" Faith said, releasing a heavy breath of air. "I had just seen Kevin, the man that I've been dating for almost a year that day outside the banquet hall kissing another woman."

"Oh, no" her friends sympathized.

"That's not the worst of it." Faith continued. "The woman was pregnant."

"What?!" her friends gasped.

"It gets worse," Faith said, dramatically holding the atomic bomb for last. "Turns out, it was his wife," she blurted out in an explosive sob.

The ladies were dumbfounded. Denise choked on her drink, spewing rum and coke over the table, as Jahel pounded her back to help her catch her breath. Melissa sat frozen, mouth agape.

"Well, I guess it's my turn," Denise said, as she shook her head, feeling the need to disclose the troubles she's been having.

"Well, to start, I have developed a really bad drinking problem that has begun to cost me a lot. I could lose everything. I'm currently fighting a court case for assault and battery after I attacked an Uber driver and his passengers on one of my drunken nights. If I'm found guilty of this incident, I may possibly have to do some jail time. It will go on my record and possibly threaten my license and my chance of being able to practice medicine," Denise said, as her voice trembled. She tried to remain strong while crying on the inside.

"Damn, DC, I'm sorry to hear that!" Faith said with sincerity as she referred to Denise using her nickname from back in college.

Jahel blurted out, pointing to herself as her eyes filled with tears, "My husband and I are having trouble conceiving a baby. When we went to see a specialist, they ran tests on us both to see what the issue may be. It turns out that I am the issue! Now they're basically saying I gotta have a test tube baby!" she said as she placed her hands on her temples and let out a soft cry.

"Everything is going to be okay!" Denise said as she immediately placed her hand on Jahel's back gently rubbing it hoping to provide some comfort.

"I did a total 180 degree change!" Melissa shouted. "I went from being the free-spirited party girl to a professional, respectable, well-mannered young lady and I'll be damned if I let another woman push me to the point where I am triggered to respond in an aggressive way. I left that part of me back in college!" She said with a little base in her voice but, this time, directing all of the energy towards herself.

"I apologize to each of you for the way I responded after the blow up at the bridal shower. You guys were only looking out for me, and I blamed you all and the liquor for giving me the courage to do something that I should have done way before the bridal shower. I feared that I would lose Stephen if I didn't accept his mom. Even when I felt he put her before me, I never said anything. So, the only person to blame for my actions on that day is me. I let things go way too far and I exploded at the wrong place and time. I definitely should have handled this situation better," Melissa said as she looked at each friend with an apologetic look on her face.

Mya sat quietly as she looked around the circular table. She could see traces of tears on each of her friends' faces as they listened to each other's stories. Mya realized that all this time, she had been trying to maintain a perfect image and keep her problems concealed, and now she was sitting in the presence of her closest friends who all seemed to have been trying to model that same image as they were all secretly suffering in silence.

At that moment, she felt that it was the perfect time for some love to be present. "Group Hug?" Mya shouted as the ladies all rose from their chairs and formed a small circle next to their table.

"I want us to promise that we will never suffer in silence again. We have each other to rely on. We are sisters for a reason!" Mya said as the ladies all held hands.

"I love you girls!" Melissa said, as they all raised their hands and pulled in for a group hug.

"We love you too!" They all responded as they bonded.

"So, wait!" Jahel said, interrupting the moment of joy. "What ever happened to the Golden Star Award?"

Mya burst into laughter. "That was actually a real part of the story that I used to get you all here. I just won't receive that honor until next month. Don't worry, you all will be invited."

"Well congratulations in advance!" Denise said as the ladies went in for another group hug!

Mya excused herself from the table as she made her way to the corridor of the restaurant to find a quiet space to take her incoming call. Once she was out of the way of listening ears, she answered.

"Hey there," Jacob replied. "So, are things okay between you and the other ladies? Have you all had a chance to talk yet?" he asked.

"Yes," Mya responded. Her response immediately gave Jacob the impression that there were definitely good vibes roaming throughout Miami. She spoke a mile a minute, sharing the details of the conversation that included laughing, crying and rejoicing."

"I'm glad things worked out!" He said after hearing the story.

"I can say the same. I was extremely nervous about how things would play out when we all met up, but it's safe to say we were able to reconcile our differences," Mya said before continuing on. "I want to thank you for being a great supporter and for providing a listening ear to this drama over the past few weeks," she expressed in an I owe you voice.

He could tell that she was wearing a big smile on her face. At that moment Mya felt the intensity of their relationship growing, she felt like they were beginning to develop a genuine bond.

"So, there's another plan I have in place that can be a great factor in resolving the remaining differences left lingering in this whole fiasco, but I'm going to need the help of you and the other ladies to pull this off." Jacob said.

Mya's antennas went up as she waited to hear more details. She sat quietly on the phone as he disclosed the ingredients of the plan. Mya listened, intrigued by Jacob's confidence, in addition to the words that were coming from his mouth. She could feel the sense of a deep connection growing between them as she analyzed his methods to end all the madness. He was becoming more impressionable as time progressed. Mya couldn't believe she had allowed herself to become so open and vulnerable with Jacob this easily after all that she had been through in her past relationship with Gibson, but for some reason this felt like a safe zone for her.

"I'm going to let you get back to your friends and I'll follow up with you later if any changes in the plan occur. You ladies continue having a good time" Jacob said, while unexpectedly relieving Mya of her inner thoughts as he brought their conversation to a close.

Mya ended the call and stood in silence looking into the distance, deep in thought. "Hey girl, is everything okay?" Melissa asked as she walked up and placed her hand on Mya's shoulder.

"Yes!" Mya responded. She turned around smiling from ear to ear secretly knowing that Melissa had no clue of what was next to come.

CHAPTER TWENTY FIVE
The Breakdown

"This is a really nice place," Jahel said to Mya as she looked around admiring the ambiance of the room and the wonderful smell of food that filled the air.

"Yeah excellent choice for brunch," Faith added to the compliment as she grabbed a champagne flute glass filled with what she believed to be a mimosa from the server's platter who was walking past.

"Everything looks so delicious" Denise said as she sat at the table joining her friends who were already seated.

"Yes, it's just as good as it looks, too!" Melissa implied while filling her face with a piece of the omelet and some of the fresh fruit from her plate. "I am so happy that we're all in a good space with each other right now," Melissa said with a warm smile on her face. She paused briefly, before she continued talking. "I just wish I could say the same for my relationship."

Determined not to become emotional at this moment, Melissa rose from her chair and excused herself. "Girl, I'm going to go get some of those cinnamon rolls" she laughed in a desperate attempt to change her emotional state. She stood and turned to walk away. When all of sudden she froze in her tracks.

The girls looked with worry while Mya had a nervous grin on her face. "Girl, what's wrong?" Denise asked. Melissa stood startled in a look of disbelief as if she had just seen a ghost. Jacqueline was standing at the entrance doorway of the room. The smile that was just once spread across Melissa's face was quickly wiped away as she prepared herself for battle. Jacqueline witnessed the instant change in Melissa's facial expression and could feel the thickness in the tension from across the way as she entered the room.

"Can we please have a moment alone to talk?" Jacqueline asked in a soft and pleasant tone.

Melissa scanned her brain for multiple ways she could respond to this question before deciding to select the mature, adult option.

"Of course, we can," she agreed while walking towards the exit of the room out into the lobby area for more privacy.

They both took a seat in plush floral-designed chairs separated by a small circle table. Jacqueline turned her body in the chair facing Melissa as she began speaking.

"I don't want to make any excuses for my previous actions, but I would like to take responsibility for them. When my husband left me for another woman, Stephen was the person who took over as the man of the house and kept everything together for me and his younger brother.

Stephen, especially when I was going through my battle with cancer, grew protective of my health and heart. I guess I grew more protective of him as well. I was afraid for him to fall hard for someone like I did with his dad, so I tried to control your relationship. I didn't want him to get hurt and end up heartbroken like I did. I know I had no right to make that decision for him. I truly owe you an apology for my behavior. I had no right to make your moment of a lifetime all about me, my emotions and selfish ways," Jacqueline said as a teardrop trickled down her face. "You are a beautiful woman and deserve nothing but the best. If you still want to marry my son, I promise to stay in my lane."

Melissa sat quietly still trying to process the words that had just come out of Jacqueline's mouth. This was the first time she had ever seen Jacqueline in such a vulnerable and humble state. She was confused and unsure how to respond.

Jacqueline leaned forward and placed both her hands on top of Melissa's and with a welcoming smile. "It would be an honor to call you my daughter in-law!"

A single tear dropped down Melissa's cheek as they both rose and embraced each other. Melissa rested her head on Jaqueline's shoulder and saw her friends eavesdropping in the doorway boohooing with joy. All of a sudden, the ladies parted from the entrance and through the door walked Stephen.

Melissa's eyes widened and her heart skipped as he stepped forward and kneeled down on one knee holding the same ring box in his hand he previously used to propose. Jacqueline moved to the side leaving Melissa standing face to face with Stephen.

"I will never make you have to question my loyalty, love or respect for you again if you will accept me as your husband one more time." he said, lifting the black box with one hand as he pulled the top of the case back revealing her beautiful diamond ring. "Melissa, will you marry me?" The entire lobby went silent as everyone stared frantically waiting for her response.

"I've never been proposed to three times!" Melissa said in a delightful tone while holding both hands to her cheeks in disbelief of what was happening. She extended her left hand, positioning her ring finger to accept his offer and yelled, "YES!" for everyone in the building to hear. The audience cheered as Melissa and Stephen kissed passionately.

CHAPTER TWENTY SIX

The Wedding Day

I can't believe this day has finally come, Melissa thought in disbelief as she stood outside on the patio deck. She looked up into the blue sky filled with marshmallow fluff clouds, as a delightful breeze swept past her body. She closed her eyes for a few seconds as she stood still, allowing the radiant rays of the sun to kiss her skin with a glowing effect.

Melissa opened her eyes and looked around. She gazed in admiration at the beautiful display she was witnessing. There on the ocean front was a tall canopy draped with white chiffon curtains and covered with beautiful red roses on each post. There were people sitting in several rows of chairs positioned facing the canopy with their backs turned to Melissa. Separating the two sections of chairs were tall posts placed at the beginning of each row. On top of the posts were large bouquets of red roses. White candles sat in the center of the arrangements. Down the middle ran a long white rug that would lead her down the aisle to her handsome king who awaited his beautiful queen.

Melissa trembled with anticipation as she held her bouquet filled with white lilies and roses accented with crystal brooches. Before she could get weak in the knees, her father walked up, stood to the right of her and smoothly cuffed his arm underneath hers, intertwining them together.

"Are you ready, baby girl?" he asked, adoring how his little girl was all grown up now.

"Yes," she replied confidently as her dad's presence brought comfort to the moment. The music began to play as Melissa's father escorted her down the aisle. Melissa glanced slightly at the people sitting by her side as she walked. The guests, who were close family and friends, made the ceremony more intimate and private just like she preferred.

Once they reached the end of the carpet, Melissa's dad turned to face her as he lifted her sheer white veil that covered her face and placed a gentle kiss on her forehead, being sure not to smudge her make-up. When he was done he walked away and took the first seat in the front row next to her mom who was wearing a smile filled with joy as she and Melissa made eye contact with each other. There before Melissa stood Stephen. They joined hands as the minister began to speak.

"Dearly beloved we are gathered here today..." he said standing before them holding a bible in his hand. Melissa was still in disbelief as this moment was really happening for her. She was marrying the love of her life on a beach front surrounded by the people she cared about the most. She was currently witnessing her fairy-tale dream fantasy wedding come to life right before her eyes.

"Melissa, do you take Stephen to be your lawfully wedded husband?" the minister asked.

"Yes! yes," she replied excitedly.

"You may kiss your bride!" The minister said giving him the lawful right to unite and celebrate their union with a kiss, while everyone clapped and shouted cheering the newlyweds on.

***

"Excuse me for a moment Aunt Erma, I need to make my way to the ladies' room," Mya said, placing her hand on Aunt Erma's arm to grasp her attention.

"Go ahead Chile!"

"I'll be here in this same spot enjoying this beautiful scene! Plus, I need to get these zip lock bags filled with my snacks for later," Aunt Erma said with a serious face as she pulled a few small plastic bags from her purse.

Mya smirked, shaking her head at Aunt Erma who sat shamelessly counting her bags for the pilfer. "I'll be right back," Mya said and rushed to the ladies room. Mya entered the bathroom and quickly made her way to the first available stall.

She sat over the toilet releasing the fluids that uncomfortably filled her bladder. As Mya stood up and arranged her dress back to the appropriate position, she heard the whimper of someone crying.

Mya opened the stall door and peeped out to see where the sound was coming from. The sound led her to the lobby area in the back of the ladies room. She found Jahel sitting on a white faux leather bench.

"Hey girl, what's wrong?" Mya asked. She took a seat on the bench and placed her arm around Jahel's shoulder. The two women sat in silence as Mya continued gently rubbing Jahel's arm to console her. The sound of two familiar voices was heard giggling as they entered the bathroom chattering with much excitement. Mya could tell from the laughter that it was Denise and Faith. She could hear the sound of their voices getting closer as they made their way to the back lobby area.

"What are you two doing back here?" asked Denise. Both ladies looked up at them but did not respond. "Remember we all agreed and promised that we would no longer keep secrets. We're here to support and help each other," said Faith.

"Perfectly stated!" Denise agreed.

Mya joined in next, "Yes, Jahel what's bothering you girl? We want to help you get through it." she said, reassuring her with a hug from the side that it was okay to share.

Jahel calmed down and began to speak. "I apologize if I startled you all, but these are actually tears of joy!" Jahel said, releasing a chuckle as she wiped the remaining tears from her eyes with the napkin in her hand.

"Oh, that's great to hear!" Denise shouted as her once concerned look turned to a smile. The other ladies began to giggle as a smile appeared on their faces as well.

"This laughter sounds like a reason to celebrate," Denise added as she reached into a fancy shopping bag she was holding and pulled out a white and gold champagne bottle.

"Okay so what's going on?" Melissa said using her famous phrase as she stood in the entryway of the lobby area with her hands on both hips displaying the curves of her waistline in her beautiful lace beaded wedding gown.

The set up of this scene gave her a feeling of Deja vu as she waited for someone in the group to respond to her question.

"Well, we were getting ready to celebrate some good news so I'm glad you're here to join us!" Denise said as she held the champagne up for display and popped the cork.

"Oh no, I will not have another repeated episode like the last one when our bathroom shenanigans took place!" Melissa said, in a playful but serious tone.

"I'm happy you said that," Denise agreed. "Because I started rehab a month ago and this is a bottle of non-alcoholic champagne," Denise said as she proudly showed off the bottle to the ladies.

"O.M.G., DC I'm so happy to hear that for you," Melissa said with a genuine smile.

"Well, I won't be drinking for a while." Jahel said as she chimed in on the topic of sobriety.

"I just received a call from my doctor and it seems that God has answered my prayers and blessed us with a miracle. I'm 4 weeks pregnant!" Jahel's eyes filled with tears again, still in disbelief. "I wasn't supposed to start my IVF treatments for another two weeks." Jahel added in shock.

"Look at God!" Mya said with joy.

"Now this is a reason to pop a bottle," Melissa said.

"Yes!" Faith added. "I have moved on with my life and I'm completely done with that liar, Kevin."

"Well, as for me" Mya said with a sneaky smile on her face looking at her friends. and continued, "I settled my unfinished business with Andre. I had my lawyer reach out to Gibson's lawyer explaining that this issue would become a legal matter if the stalking persisted. As for me and Jacob, we've been really getting to know each other more and we both like what each other have to offer," she said with a devilish smile, giving her girls the, "you-know-what" look.

"Okayy!" Denise said as she took a swig of the non-alcoholic champagne.

"I would like to raise a toast!" Melissa said, snatching the bottle from Denise. "This has been an amazingly rocky experience, but it has not only taught us a lot about each other, it taught us a lot about ourselves and brought us all closer together as well. Thanks, Mya, for always being so dope. This wouldn't have happened without you," Melissa said looking in Mya's direction.

Melissa took a swig of the bottle and passed it to Mya. Mya smiled with gratitude, lifted the bottle and saluted, "To building a stronger sisterhood and congratulations to Mrs. Melissa Sinclair-Scott!"

They all joined in cheering with excitement passing the bottle from hand to hand. The bathroom echoed with laughter, jokes and reveries as they passed the bottle, just like their last night in their college apartment.

The End...